Best wishes,

Nowhere to Run

Jeanne Bannon

~ Acclaim for Jeanne Bannon ~

For *Invisible*

"Absorbing, warm and occasionally playful—the story of a young woman whose invisibility helps her to better see herself, and helps others to see who she really is."
—*Kirkus Reviews*

"...[A] great story... The lessons are valuable and uplifting."
—*The Kindle Book Review*

Copyright Warning

Copyright © 2015 by Jeanne Bannon

Published by: Blueberry Hill Press, 2015
ISBN 978-0-9940825-1-0

~ Dedication ~

For Nina, my best friend, the light of my life.
For Sara, my miracle, my treasure.

Acknowledgments

This book would not have come to fruition if it had not been for a writing challenge of a few years ago. I'd like to say thank you to the women who I'd started the process with, even though I ended up leaving to do my own thing. You lit a fire under me and gave me the fuel and motivation to make my vision a reality.

Thank you to Sheila Dalton, my right hand, my cheerleader, and, a dear friend. The book would not be what it is today without your input and amazing editorial eye.

Thank you to Georgina Richardson for being one of the best beta readers I've ever had. You've added so much to the story.

Thanks also to Luigina Leonelli for your help during those first drafts. Through thick and thin, sick and sin.

I am grateful to my husband, Dave, for his unwavering belief in me. I'm also grateful to my parents for leaving books around the house when I was growing up. Books I picked up and read voraciously. Thanks for making me a reader, which in turn made me a writer.

CHAPTER 1

The ghosts of those we love never leave us. They live on in our hearts but break them too, Lily thought as she flipped the sign on the door of the Higgstown Diner from "Open" to "Closed." Then she sank wearily onto a stool at the counter, finally at the end of the workday. Now she could let loose the heaviness weighing her down. Hot tears stung her eyes and she let them. It was OK. There was no one around to witness her breakdown. She rested her head in her hands and heaved with sobs.

"Sara, please talk to me. Give me a sign you're still around," Lily said to the air. "I miss you so much." More tears washed down her cheeks. It had been three months since her sister's death, and there was still no escaping Sara's ghost. Even the chipped Arborite counter where she now sat, with the wonky red upholstered stool that swiveled just a little too much to the right, brought back memories. Lily could see her older sister as plainly as if she were standing in front of her now, black hair piled high in a bun and that blue eye shadow she was so fond of. Lily smiled through her tears.

Sara had been a whiz at the grill, whipping up orders faster than Lily ever could. God, how long had the diner been a part of their lives? More than twenty-five years, she guessed. They were just kids when their mother, Nancy, bought the place—Lily, seven, and Sara, twelve.

A creak came from the back of the diner. Lily lifted her head to listen. Another small groan of the floorboards. Could Sara be giving her a sign?

"Sara?" Lily slid off the stool.

A tall, dark figure loomed in the doorway.

Lily froze, her heart near exploding. "What do you want?" she choked out in a thin voice.

He stepped nearer. "Open the register." His voice was a deep whisper.

A balaclava hid his face; the seams of a dark gray coat strained over a thickly muscled physique. He aimed the gun in his right hand at her chest.

Her feet seemed rooted to the floor.

"I said, open the register."

The man moved close enough for Lily to catch his scent—a mix of sweat and cheap aftershave. He shoved her forward, snapping her from her stupor, and followed as she made her way behind the counter to the cash register.

A glowing red light caught her attention. She hadn't turned off the coffee maker! In one quick movement, Lily grabbed the pot's plastic handle and launched the scorching brew at the woolen knit of the intruder's balaclava. The gun landed with a thud between his booted feet as he clawed at the steaming mask plastered to his face.

Now was her chance. Lily shouldered past him to the front door. Her fingers, thick and clumsy with panic, fumbled as she tried in vain to turn the two deadbolt locks. She ordered herself to calm down. Take a breath. C'mon, you can do this, she told herself, but her heart jack hammered in her chest, and her ears pulsed with the rush of blood behind them.

Suddenly, a face appeared on the other side of the glass front door of the diner, sending Lily backward, nearly tripping over her own feet.

The stranger on the other side of the door took her in. A look of confusion flickered across his face. Then, as if coming back to himself, he yelled, "Hurry. Unlock the door!" The cold night air whipped his dark hair wildly around his face. His pale blue eyes locked on hers.

Panic had hijacked her brain. She didn't know what to do. He could be an accomplice.

"Turn around," the stranger yelled and gestured with a twirl of his finger. What else could she do? There was no other option, so she did as he said and moved into a corner, keeping a careful eye on the burglar who, oddly, seemed just as anchored in place as she was.

The sudden crash of shattered glass made Lily turn back around to see the stranger reaching through the broken pane, unlocking the door.

"You OK?" he asked, stepping inside.

Lily nodded, unsure if he was friend or foe. Her wide-eyed gaze turned to the burglar, who was now approaching. He hadn't fled as she'd hoped.

"Call the cops," the stranger said.

The men were a few feet from each other. Her rescuer bent to scoop up the gun, but a knee caught him square in the chest, knocking him backward. The other man lunged for the weapon.

Lily grabbed for the metal umbrella stand near the door and upended it, sending a mosaic of unclaimed and forgotten umbrellas crashing to the floor. With one quick heft, she whacked the intruder across the back with ten pounds of brass, making a crack so loud she was amazed to see him still upright. He groaned and threw her a menacing glare. The blow hadn't been enough to fell him, but it did buy them some time. Her rescuer barreled into the burglar, slamming him to the wall with a skull-cracking thud.

The way to the phone behind the counter was finally clear. Lily punched in 911 with shaky fingers. The operator on the other end began to ask questions she didn't have time to answer. "Three twenty-six Maple Ridge Drive, Higgstown Diner. Hurry!" was all she said before running back over to help.

"Rope, duct tape, anything?" the stranger asked. He had the burglar in a headlock, and although the man looked unconscious, Lily was afraid he'd come to at any moment.

"In the back." She was off and returned a moment later with a roll of silver-gray tape.

"Name's Aiden by the way." He flashed a dimpled smile, and Lily felt her legs go weak. How was it she was just noticing his good looks? The whole scene was ridiculous, and she had to stifle an urge to laugh. Here was a gorgeous guy, smiling at her, with his arm wrapped like a vice around some thug's neck.

"Lily," she replied, coming back to herself.

"Lily, can you manage to wrap some of that tape around his wrists?"

She nodded.

"Then do it, quick."

She moved nimbly, her hands not as shaky now that Aiden was with her. Lily made quick work of securing the man's wrists, noticing how thick they were and the fact his hands were rough and calloused. Next, she moved to his ankles, wrapping the tape around his legs above the tops of his well-worn leather hiking boots until the roll was almost used up. Finally, she smacked a rectangle of tape over his mouth, which wasn't easy to do since he'd screwed his face into a grimace, and all the while stared at her through hooded eyes. She'd brushed the reddish stubble on his cheek, making her cringe and reflexively wipe her hand on her apron.

Aiden released the man, who slumped bonelessly to the floor. His eyes were open now, and he wriggled and grunted in an effort to free himself. With a swift kick, Aiden sent the gun sailing across the dingy gray linoleum to the far end of the diner.

"He'll be fine till the cops get here." Aiden's voice and demeanor were as calm as if he rescued damsels in distress every day. With a gentle hand on her elbow, he led Lily to a booth at the front of the diner. "Why don't we wait here?"

She sat, shivering as the cold night air streamed in through the open door. All she had on was her short-sleeved uniform, and gooseflesh pricked her skin. Aiden took off his jacket and wrapped it around her.

She took him in as he sat opposite her. "Thanks."

He was big, at least as tall as the burglar, and broader, with hair the color of rich dark earth and pale blue eyes that shone like robin's eggs against his olive complexion. And he had a dimple, just one, in his right cheek. Despite the danger no more than ten feet away, Lily had never felt safe.

"I guess the sheriff's on his way," she said, eyeing the writhing intruder. "You sure the tape will hold?"

"Yup. You did a great job. Almost like you've done this before." A brow shot up in mock accusation.

Despite the chill, a flush rose to her cheeks and she looked away.

He suddenly seemed contrite. "Are you all right? I mean you just went through quite an ordeal."

"I...I'm OK." She wanted to say more, but he was a stranger. How could she tell him her problems? How could she say this bungled burglary was the least of her worries?

He looked around. "This your place?"

Everything's mine now that my sister and mother are dead, she was tempted to say, but what came out was simply, "Yeah, it's all mine." Lily got up and went over to a cupboard behind the counter and grabbed a bottle of Scotch and two glasses.

"I'm sorry, but I really need this." A flicker of a smile came and went as she poured an inch of the amber liquid with a trembling hand and sat. Aiden took the bottle from her and finished pouring his own drink.

She downed hers, coughed, and covered her mouth with the back of her hand.

Aiden knocked back his Scotch, then poured another for each of them.

The liquor warmed her, and soon sweet abandon swept her away. Cares drifted, and even the bound man on the floor was no longer a concern.

A red, pulsing glow filled the diner with large swooping circles.

"Sheriff's here." Lily rose and held onto the back of the seat for support. Then shrugged off the jacket and handed it back to Aiden. The cool air was refreshing now that she was warmed by liquor.

He followed her to the door and stood close behind. She had the feeling he wanted to wrap an arm protectively around her shoulder, and part of her wished he would.

Sheriff Royce Wilkins, a slender, drooping black man, ducked through the empty door frame, his lips pressed into a grim line as he threw a nod at Lily.

With arms crossed tightly over her chest, she nodded back.

Wilkins eyed the man on the floor, who now lay still. An eyebrow shot up in a question mark as he turned his attention to Aiden.

"This is Aiden. He helped me," Lily said.

Aiden held out a hand. "Aiden O'Rourke."

Wilkins shook it. "Mr. O'Rourke, looks like you were in the right place at the right time."

"Yes, he was," Lily answered for him.

"You OK, Lily?" The sheriff bent down beside the intruder and ripped the duct tape from his mouth with one quick flick.

"Fine."

The man groaned and whipped his head from side to side, as if trying to wipe away the pain. A rectangle of angry, red flesh glowed where the tape had been.

The sheriff plucked the coffee-soaked balaclava from the floor and pulled a plastic baggie from his jacket pocket. After dropping the mask inside, he sealed it. "Looks like someone got a face full of steaming hot coffee. That your doing, Lily?"

She nodded but didn't say anything.

Wilkins turned to Aiden. "Mind givin' me a hand?" He tipped his head toward the intruder. Wilkins grabbed an arm, and Aiden was quick to follow. Together, they heaved the burglar to his feet.

"Gun's over there," Aiden said, nodding toward the back of the diner as the sheriff began his pat down.

Wilkins pulled a knife from the man's jacket. Holding it between a gloved thumb and forefinger, he deposited it into another baggie. "No wallet? No ID? Looks like you were up to no good."

The man kept silent, his lips pressed into a line of discontent.

Deputy Antonio Deluca ducked through the broken pane of the door and surveyed the scene. Short, in his mid-thirties with a wispy black moustache, he wore the look of a man who'd rather be on the couch watching the game than doing his job.

"Fetch the gun. It's at the back," the sheriff said to his deputy without taking his eyes from his charge. "You gotta name?"

"I ain't sayin' nothin' till I see a lawyer."

"Thought as much." Wilkins pushed up the sleeves of the man's jacket before unclipping his handcuffs from his belt and slapping them onto the burglar's wrists. Then he pulled a penknife from his pocket and sliced through the duct tape.

Antonio was back with the gun. "Bag that and take this nice young man to the station and book him," the sheriff said.

CHAPTER 2

Aiden stayed to help the sheriff secure the broken front door with a few scraps of plywood they'd scrounged from a back room. It should be good enough to hold until morning when Lily would be able to call for a repairman.

Lily left shortly afterward, and though Aiden was a willing escort, she insisted on driving herself home. Brave woman and goddamn resourceful. He admired her but still cringed when he thought of what his man, Chrome, had had to endure that evening. Poor bastard, done in by a pot of decaf. Aiden would probably have to pay him extra— danger pay. He laughed at the thought. It really was kinda funny. Lily was more than he'd bargained for—a hellcat of a redhead—and probably would have been able to handle Chrome without his help.

Now that Lily was out of earshot, Wilkins fixed Aiden with a death stare. "What the hell are you up to, Aiden?"

Aiden looked around and tapped his cell. "Give me a minute to get to my car."

He slid behind the wheel of his truck in the parking lot of the Higgstown Diner and fished his already ringing phone from his pocket.

"OK, so what the hell did you do?" came the voice on the other end.

Aiden smirked. "My job."

The sheriff wasted no time getting to the point. "Your guy spilled. Told us about your arrangement. That's not what we'd planned." Agitation colored Wilkins's voice.

"I couldn't explain with Lily right there, and it was a brilliant way to meet the lovely and charming Ms. Valier in person, don't you think? Bet I've made quite the impression."

"You were supposed to lie low for a few days before making contact," the sheriff chided. "Makes me doubt my decision to bring you in on this. Tell me you're not a loose cannon, Aiden."

Aiden smiled. He wanted to laugh but had no intention of digging himself in deeper. He was the man police departments around the country hired when their investigations hit a brick wall. Especially ones like this—small-town sheriff and only one deputy with homicide experience.

"Lily's quite a looker, sheriff." Of course, he'd seen pictures in her file before he'd actually met her, but they hadn't done her justice. Yet it was more than Lily's beauty that caught Aiden's attention back there in the diner. It was how she carried herself. So feminine and seductive without even trying—the way her hands, with their long, tapered fingers, moved so elegantly.

The sheriff was quick to respond, "Don't go fallin' for that woman. Ya hear me? Keep it official. Just get the proof we need to put her away."

"I know why I'm here."

"You met Lily and now she thinks you're a hero, but what the hell am I supposed to do with that guy you hired? What's his name?"

Aiden laughed. "Street name's Chrome, but his real name's Dave. Can you house him in your jail for a night? I'll stop by to pay him and then he can get outta town tomorrow." Aiden didn't wait for a reply. "Anyway, thanks for your help with this. I'd better get back to the cabin. That is if I can find the damn thing in the dark. Could you have found me anything *more* secluded? I feel like a freaking mountain man in that place."

"Shit," was all the sheriff said before hanging up.

Aiden gave his phone a wry smile then tucked it back into his jeans. Guess he'd be a city boy masquerading as a country bumpkin for a while, but he was glad for the challenge.

He took another glance at the Higgstown Diner before driving away.

* * *

Aiden's new home was an authentic log cabin. How long he'd be in town he didn't know, but what did it matter? There was no one back home in Chicago waiting for him, not even a pet. He was accountable to no one and liked it that way.

Aiden got to work building a fire in the huge stone fireplace and soon had a roaring blaze. He found a coffee maker in a cupboard, brewed a cup of java, grabbed hold of his beaten-up leather travel bag, and settled onto the couch to enjoy his handiwork. A niggling voice reminded him just how nice it would be to share this moment with someone special. "Aw, shut up," he said aloud and stuffed the thought away.

He unzipped the bag and pulled out his files. It took a moment to find the one he wanted—an old case involving a woman who'd skipped town with her eight-year-old daughter, dropping everything to get away from her abusive husband. Her name was Connie. Aiden had been hired by Connie's mother to find her before her shithead of a husband, or the cops, did.

His heart tore in two every time he thought of the case. It was the only one he'd failed at. The only one where the bad guy beat him. Looking now at the picture of a smiling Connie and her little girl, he felt the warmth of tears begin to form in his eyes and pinched them away. Never, he vowed, never would he screw up a case again.

Morning came too quickly, and Aiden awoke bundled up on the couch. He hadn't bothered to go up to the bedroom loft, just pulled the throw from the back of the couch over himself and nodded off. He'd slept in his clothes and was grateful he'd had the presence of mind to toe off his boots first.

An uncomfortable gurgling in his stomach sent him to the kitchen in search of food, but he'd only bought a few things at the corner store when he hit town. He thought of Lily and the diner. Should he go back so soon? He was torn between duty and a niggling desire to see Lily again. He should do some surveillance first—watch her a bit, but then again, having a little chat with Miss Valier may prove valuable too.

After a little freshening up, he pulled into a parking space in front of the diner. A pudgy, middle-aged man in an untucked flannel shirt and dirty jeans was hard at work replacing the broken glass of the front door.

Aiden entered. Even the chill of the October air sweeping in through the empty doorway hadn't kept customers away. Probably die-hard regulars. A smile unfurled across his face as the smells of frying bacon and fresh coffee swept past him, making his stomach gurgle and rumble. Customers, perched at the counter and in booths, were bundled in their coats, shoveling eggs, toast, and crispy bacon into their mouths.

After finding a spot at the counter, he looked around for Lily but saw only a harried, middle-aged waitress making her rounds with a coffee pot in each hand, one orange-rimmed, the other brown. Bangs, just a little too long, bounced up and down with her eyelids, which were covered thickly with glittery silver-and-purple eye shadow.

"Mornin'," she said as she made her way to the business side of the counter. "What can I getcha?"

"Coffee, please." Aiden read her nametag. "You the only one working today, Annie?"

She turned over the cup resting in a saucer in front of him. "Nah, Lily's here. She's just in back. Can I getcha anything else?"

Aiden pulled a sticky, plastic-covered menu from its place between the ketchup and saltshaker. It took only a second to find what he wanted. "I'll have the lumberjack special." He pointed at the accompanying picture of three pancakes, four eggs, a mountain of home fries, and five strips of bacon.

"Sure thing," Annie said with a lingering gaze, her eyes narrowing just a bit. "You're new around here, aren't ya?" She waited a moment before turning toward the grill to start his order.

"Yeah," Aiden answered, then swiveled around looking for Lily. Just as he did, she stepped from the back, arms filled with what looked like bags of frozen home fries. Aiden jumped to his feet and ran to help, taking them from her.

"Oh, hi," Lily said with a startled smile. Her green eyes were even more beautiful in the light of day.

"Where do you want these?"

"Counter's fine."

Aiden walked back to where he'd been sitting and placed the surprisingly heavy, and very cold, bags of potatoes on the counter.

"Thanks." Lily touched his shoulder as she passed.

Though he couldn't feel the heat of her touch through his jacket, his skin tingled anyway. He had to remind himself to stay focused on the business at hand.

Lily began helping Annie at the grill, plucking small order sheets from the overhead carousel.

"So, looks like business is still booming," Aiden said.

Lily turned to face him and offered a warm smile. "You're right about that." She took a quick glimpse at the black plastic clock over the door. "If you stick around for about half an hour, things should slow down. Then we can talk, that is, if you'd like." She suddenly seemed shy.

Aiden nodded and raised his cup in a salute. "I'd like that very much." He wouldn't have been able to put away his smile if he wanted to.

CHAPTER 3

The rhythms of the diner were as much a part of Lily as the red of her hair and the green of her eyes. She'd called it right. Within thirty minutes, the restaurant held a manageable four customers. There were a few hours until the lunch rush, so she invited Aiden to a booth and asked Annie to take over.

Aiden pulled out his wallet to pay his bill, but Lily waved him off. "No, after what you did for me last night, it's on the house." She smiled. "It's the least I can do."

He tipped his head in a gesture of thanks. "I appreciate it, though it's completely unnecessary." Wagging a finger, he said, "Don't be doing this every time I come in, OK?"

They slid into the same booth they'd sat in the night before. What a difference a day makes, she thought, eyeing him. Today her heart was hammering for a very different reason. The only danger now was that this handsome stranger just might steal her heart if she wasn't careful.

"You gotta deal, mister. The way you eat, I'd go broke in a month." She let out a throaty laugh and was immediately self-conscious. He smiled and stared at her with…what? Admiration? She couldn't tell for sure but found herself smoothing her hair and wishing she'd put on lipstick.

A disappointing thought suddenly struck her. He was new in town, so maybe he was just passing through. The words slipped from her thoughts and out of her mouth. "What brings you to town?"

"Thinking of starting a business."

She straightened and tried to hold back the smile about to erupt on her lips. "Here, in Higgstown? What kind, if you don't mind me asking?"

He tented his fingers and looked thoughtful. "Oh, I don't know, maybe a little souvenir shop. I hear it gets really busy during the tourist season. I'm retired and don't need the income. Just want something to keep me out of trouble."

He looked to be in his mid-thirties. How odd to be retired so young. "So, you'd be staying here? For good, I mean?" She cringed inwardly, hating how lame and desperate she sounded.

A smile lit his face as if he'd caught her meaning. "More than likely. If I can manage to set something up."

An errant lock of hair fell over his forehead, and it took all the self-control she could muster not to brush it back in place. "This probably isn't the best time of year to start a business. Summer would be better, but then again, if you're in no hurry, the scenery with the fall colors is breathtaking." She looked away, wanting to kick herself for saying it was a bad time to start a business. What did she want to do, run him off?

"I like the scenery that's in front of me right now," he said, grinning broadly.

The heat of embarrassment reddened her cheeks, and an awkward silence fell between them. Aiden reached out, stopping just short of touching her hand. "Sorry. I didn't mean to..."

"No, no...you didn't do anything to be sorry for."

"What I'm trying to do is ask you out, and so far I'm not doing a very good job of it."

Lily's brows lifted with interest. It wasn't as if she hadn't been asked out before. Every unattached guy in town had hit on her at one time or another and a few of the married ones too, but this guy was different. She didn't have to worry about his motives. He was new in Higgstown and didn't yet know how much she was worth.

She loved the scruff on his chiseled jawline and that dimple! It was cavernous, and he didn't even have to smile for it to pop.

"So, what do you think? Would you like to go out with me tonight?" He leaned closer to catch her gaze.

"I'd love to," she replied with more fervor than intended.

His smile split his face. "Great. When do you get off work?"

Lily pulled her order pad and pen from her apron pocket and wrote down her number and address on the back of a sheet. "I'm off at six." She slid the paper to him, and when their fingers met, a sizzle of electricity shot up her arm.

* * *

Six o'clock came quickly, and Lily was out the door. Unusual for her, but the thought of seeing Aiden and knowing she didn't have much time to get ready lit a fire under Lily. Denise, tall, scrawny, and still sporting pimples at twenty-four, was working the evening shift. Lily barely said two words to the poor girl before hurrying out. Normally, she'd stop and chat for a while but not tonight.

Her stomach fluttered with excitement as she got into her car and turned up the tunes. Before she realized it, she was singing—that was something she hadn't done in some time. However, it wasn't long before the dark thoughts sneaked up on her as they often did. Hell, why was she always punishing herself whenever a little happiness entered her life? She deserved some good fortune— probably more than most people after the ordeal she'd lived through, well, was *still* living through.

She clicked off the radio, her mind turning back to the morning of Wednesday, July 13, the day her world was turned upside down. She'd been on her way out the door, heading for work, when Sheriff Wilkins met her in the driveway. She'd smiled up at him.

The tall, wiry man had cleared his throat, then adjusted his hat. "Lily, may I have a word?"

"Yes, of course. What is it? Has something happened?" Blood had rushed to her temples and pounded there. She knew the look of a man who was about to deliver bad news.

He'd nodded toward the front door. "Mind if we go inside?" His tone had been as gaunt as he was.

Lily could barely move, but she'd willed herself forward with the sheriff trailing her into the kitchen.

"Please, sit down," Lily offered and had taken a seat herself. She'd pressed her hands between her knees to keep them from shaking. Why was she so frightened? Instinct had nagged her, pressing every fear trigger she'd honed over her lifetime. Something was terribly wrong.

Wilkins had stared at her. Lily had watched him and tried to read his expression to gauge what was coming. He'd taken a seat and removed his hat, setting it on the table. "I'm afraid I have some bad news. Your sister's been found dead."

The gravity of his words had struck like a punch to the gut, and sucked the breath from her. Her world had gone black, and the last thing she'd heard before fainting had been the furious beating of her own heart.

By the time Lily got home, she'd managed, with some difficulty, to push the dark thoughts back into the recesses of her mind. Rex, her Irish terrier, clawed at the other side of the door as she turned the key in the lock and opened it.

"There's my boy," she said, bending to pet him. He was a quiet dog, never really barked, but somehow he always knew when she'd be home, even though her hours were never routine.

After taking Rex out to do his business and emptying a can of dog food into his bowl, Lily went upstairs to hit the shower. Aiden had said he'd be by at seven. That didn't leave a lot of time for preening. She kept her shower short, and when she came out of the bathroom, Rex was waiting, curled up in his bed in the corner of her room.

"Hi, my little man. How's my boy tonight?"

The dog stood and wagged his short reddish-brown tail excitedly.

"Mommy's got a date." She knelt beside him and kissed the top of his head. "Sorry to leave you again." Despite her excitement, she felt a pang of guilt. Poor Rex had been alone all day, and now here she was going out at night. With a heavy sigh, Lily ran a hand through her damp hair. "Ah, hell, I need to get a life." She eyed her dog again. "You understand, don't ya?"

Rex wagged his tail as if in reply.

"I promise not to be too late."

After blow-drying her hair and applying her makeup, she realized she didn't know where Aiden was taking her. She hadn't bothered to ask and he hadn't said. Padding to her closet, she threw open the door and took inventory. She didn't know what to wear. What would pass as a date in Higgstown, Maine? A movie, dinner, bowling? The last one she didn't much care for.

God, how she wished Sara was around to give advice. It was unbelievable how complicated her life was now. Wilkins and Deluca were the enemy. How strange that felt, to be on the other side of the law, to be looked at with suspicion. Wilkins especially was a disappointment. He'd known her since she was a child. How could he think it possible she would murder the only person in her life she loved?

Lily shook the bad thoughts away again. At least her restaurant was still in business. She'd been afraid she'd lose customers, but hers was the only diner in town. When people's stomachs got to rumblin', they came just as before. Business was business, she guessed, and friendship another matter entirely.

"What do you think of this?" Lily said aloud, pretending her sister was standing beside her, knowing she sounded like she was off her rocker. But she really did believe Sara could hear her. She yanked a pair of khaki chinos off a hanger along with a blousy cotton top. "Should be good enough for bowling, dinner, or a movie."

The crunching of tires on gravel caught her attention, and she peeked out her bedroom window in time to spy a silver Dodge Ram kicking up dust as it made its way along the meandering driveway.

Her heart took off in a sprint. She told herself to settle down between calming breaths. He was just a man for crying out loud. She took one last glance in the mirror and smiled at her reflection before heading downstairs to answer the doorbell that would ring any second.

CHAPTER 4

Before exiting the truck, Aiden punched in Wilkins's number on his cell.

The sheriff answered on the second ring. "Whatcha got for me?"

"What? No hello? Straight to business?" Aiden said.

"Damn right. That's why I hired ya."

"I'm in Lily's driveway right now. I'm taking her out and just wanted to know how hard to push. You know her better than I do, and I don't want to mess up right out of the gate."

"That's it? That's why you called? Hell, man, feel her out, push as hard as necessary to get the truth out of her. Did she kill her sister, or is she involved in any way in her sister's death? That's what we need to know." His tone held a touch of impatience.

Aiden felt the hot flush of embarrassment in his cheeks. What possessed him to ask such a stupid question?

He sighed. There was something about Lily that made him draw back a bit, like he had to be careful with her, like he didn't want to hurt her. He'd have to push those feelings aside, and quickly, if he was going to do his job.

"OK. I hear ya." Aiden cleared his throat. "How's Chrome? If he's hurt, tell him I'm sorry. I'll come by later and pay him. Guess he'd like his 'get out of jail free card' now."

"Don't worry about it—already paid him. Figured you'd be charging the department for his services anyway. He's on his way back into whatever gutter he crawled out from."

Aiden laughed. "Thanks, sheriff. Hope he didn't overcharge you."

"Guy like that can't be trusted. I gave him half of what he asked for, and he seemed happy enough."

"You're a smart man," Aiden said, relieved he didn't have to stop by the station later that evening. More time with Lily. "All right then, I'd better get going. Can't keep a lady waiting. I'll check in when I have something for you."

Aiden took a breath and readied himself for the role he was about to play. If he hadn't been a private investigator, he could've easily been an actor, but he'd decided to take the practical road, the one more frequently traveled, and went into law enforcement. After ten years on the force in Chicago, even the steady pay, benefits, and pension weren't enough to keep him at a job that was more paperwork than police work. He left, hung a shingle, and started his PI business three years ago. With cutbacks and the poor economy, police departments ended up being his best customers. Outsourcing was his cash cow. He fancied himself a freelance cop, which was perfect. There was intrigue, danger, and excitement without the tedious paperwork and red tape.

Aiden headed for the front door of Lily's restored turn-of-the-century farmhouse. Nice place. Lots of property, well kept, but not what he'd expected of someone with as much money as Miss Valier. With her millions, she should be living in a mansion with servants and have a winter home in Palm Springs. Why did she stay in small-town America and work in a crappy diner? He knew she owned it, but with the freedom her money afforded, why would she choose to keep working there? Perhaps because it had only been a few months since she'd inherited her sister's money, and she hadn't had the time to spend it yet?

He knocked on the large cherry-red door, heard what sounded like a dog on the other side, not barking or growling, but scratching, and then the door swung wide.

Aiden thought back to the photos of Lily in the file Wilkins had given him. Stress and strain were written all over that face. Hooded eyes, dark and swollen, hair hanging limply, and a forehead creased with worry. They must have been taken shortly after her sister's murder, because this woman, the one standing in front of him right now, was hot!

"Hi, come on in," Lily said, a smile playing on her lips.

She was breathtaking in her simplicity, and he wanted nothing more than to just admire her. Silky auburn hair fell over her shoulders, tempting him to reach out and run his fingers through it. When she opened the door wider, he realized he hadn't moved. He laughed and stepped inside.

The dog sniffed tentatively at his boots. "Who's this fella?" Aiden bent to pet him.

"That's Rex." She crinkled her nose. "I know, it's not a terribly original name, but he just looked like a Rex to me."

The dog jumped up on Aiden, his tail motoring from side to side. "I love dogs." He scratched behind Rex's ears. "Are you a good boy?" The dog happily lapped up the attention and gave Aiden a few slobbery kisses.

"OK, that's enough, Rex. Go, go on now. Go to bed," Lily scolded and off he went, nails clicking on the hardwood.

"Aw, you didn't have to do that. I really do love dogs."

Aiden looked around. From what he could see, she lived simply. No fancy furnishings, no polished marble floors, just old-fashioned hardwood, worn from years of use. There was barely any furniture in the living room, just a big comfy-looking easy chair by the window and a couple of bookcases jam-packed with novels.

"So, where are we going?" Lily asked. "Ready to go now, or did you want to come in for a bit?"

Aiden glanced at his watch. "It's a surprise. We'd better get going."

Lily's brows lifted with interest, but she said nothing as she grabbed a jacket from the hall closet. He helped her put it on. Her hair smelled like apples and her perfume like a lilac bush in full bloom.

"So you're really not going to tell me where we're going?" Lily asked as they made their way to Aiden's truck.

"Nope, but I'm glad you've got that nice warm jacket on." He opened the door and helped her climb in.

She turned to face him with eyes the size of poker chips and he chuckled. "Don't worry, it's not like we're going skiing or dog sledding. I'll give you a hint. Think about what time of year it is, OK?" He closed the door and smiled at her through the tinted window before getting in the driver's side.

"There's not much to do in Higgstown," she said, "so if I were to guess, I'd say either a movie or bowling."

"Remember my hint? Your nice warm jacket? Besides, I'd never take a woman *bowling* on a first date. What do you take me for?" He gave her his mock hurt face before throwing the truck into reverse and backing out onto the road.

After a couple more guesses, each crazier than the one before, she finally gave up.

"Guess you'll just have to wait and see then. In the meantime, why don't you tell me about yourself?"

Her gaze fell to her hands. "There's not much to tell. I'd bore you."

She was lying. There was a lot to tell, and he certainly wouldn't be bored. In fact, he'd be all ears, might even pull over so he could take notes. "Oh, come on. I doubt that. I told you a little about myself yesterday. Now it's your turn. Brothers and sisters?"

"Huh?"

"Do you have any brothers or sisters?"

"Oh…no. I mean, I used to. I had a sister, but she…she passed away." Her voice dipped into sadness, catching at the end.

He'd summoned up hurt. At least that's what he thought it was. Then again, it could be guilt or regret.

"I'm sorry to hear that. I didn't mean to touch on such a painful subject—"

"It's OK." She smiled halfheartedly. "Her name was Sara. She was my older sister. I just miss her is all."

"Is it OK if I ask how she died? I…I don't mean to pry; it's just that she must have been young."

"Thirty-six." Lily glanced at him and he saw tears. "She was murdered just a few months ago."

"Murdered!" Aiden injected surprise into his voice. "Oh my God, Lily, I'm so sorry." He cupped her hands with his right hand. "It couldn't have happened in Higgstown, could it? I mean this seems like such a safe place."

Lily heaved a sigh. "First murder in twenty-three years."

"Did they catch the killer?"

"Ha! The idiots who masquerade as cops around here are barely able to write speeding tickets. They're muddling the investigation. Didn't even secure the scene before dusting for prints. All the evidence they collected was inadmissible. No, they haven't caught the murderer."

Sheriff Wilkins hadn't mentioned that little tidbit when Aiden asked about prints. Only said they hadn't found any.

He took note of the venom in Lily's voice though, then forced a little optimism into his. "I'm sure they'll get to the bottom of it."

"Don't be." She was looking out the window now, her face turned away from him.

"Was there any sign of a forced entry?"

"It wasn't a robbery. Whoever killed my sister was someone she knew."

"Really? Who do you think…"

A steely look was all it took to get Aiden to switch gears. He knew when he was headed down a dead end and pushing the boundaries just a little too hard.

"Hope you don't mind eating in a diner. I would've taken you somewhere nicer, but we've got to be quick if we're going to make it to the surprise. I bet you're sick of it, diner food, I mean."

"Actually, no, not at all. I don't get to eat a meal in my restaurant all that often. I grab a bite here and there, but I never sit down and actually eat like a customer does, so, believe it or not, that sounds like a real treat."

Aiden smiled. "Good, 'cause we're here."

The Riverside Diner was bigger and a little newer than Lily's place, but this diner wasn't nearly as busy. That made her smile. Riverside was the competition despite the fact it was located twenty-five minutes away, in another town.

They were shown to their seats and handed menus by a woman well past middle age whose nametag read "Elvira." Everything about the woman was gray, from her hair to her uniform to her sensible shoes. When they sat, Elvira filled their coffee mugs without being asked, then deposited a handful of creamers from an apron pocket onto the table between the cups and disappeared, only to return a moment later, order pad in hand, pen poised.

"What'll it be?" she asked, staring out the window, her voice as flat as the pancakes on the breakfast menu.

Aiden leaned back and gestured for Lily to order first.

"Caesar salad with grilled chicken, please." She closed the menu and handed it to Elvira.

Aiden ordered a mountain burger and mashed potatoes. Lily couldn't help but giggle. The thought of a hamburger with mashed potatoes was like ordering a steak with a side of Jell-O.

"What are you laughing about?" he asked, grinning. "Is it the mashed potatoes? At least they're healthier than fries." He wagged a finger.

Lily raised a brow. "I don't know about that. Did you forget I *own* a diner? The mashed potatoes aren't exactly fresh. They're powdered and then reconstituted."

Aiden made a face and held up a hand. "Hold on right there. You're ruining my illusion of some sweet old lady toiling away in the kitchen, whipping up a fresh batch of fluffy white spuds."

Absently, she grabbed his hand and smiled. "I'm sorry. I don't want to kill your dreams. You just go right ahead and think what you like." A rush of excitement ran through her when she realized they were touching. Lily had taken his hand so naturally it was as if she'd done it a thousand times before. She peeked down at their intertwined fingers, and then her gaze rose to his eyes.

She tried to pull free, but before she could, he covered her hand with his free one. His were large and masculine. The hands of a man she knew could keep her safe.

"Any word from the sheriff on the guy who tried to rob you?"

Her stomach knotted with the question. She wasn't sure whether it was the mention of Sheriff Wilkins or the burglar that caused the distress. "No, and I probably won't hear anything. Wilkins and that deputy of his, well, let's just say we're not seeing eye to eye at the moment." She rolled her eyes then laughed. "I'm not giving you a good impression of Higgstown, am I?"

"Are you kidding? I love the town, but I'm not so sure I'd like it as much if you weren't in it."

Truth was she liked Higgstown a whole lot more now too. She went to that "what if" place in her mind. The place she usually kept under lock and key. What if he did stick around and they got close? What if he found out about the money or, worse, what if he heard the rumors? The ones people whispered behind her back and thought didn't get back to her; the rumor that was actually true—she was being investigated for the murder of her own sister. What then? He'd leave town, that's what.

"Do you mind if I ask why the bad blood between you and the sheriff?"

She hadn't said "bad blood," only that they weren't seeing eye to eye.

"We were friendly before my sister was killed. I'm just not crazy about how he and Deputy Deluca are handling the investigation. That's all."

"Does he give you updates?"

Lily drew in a sharp breath. Maybe one day she could tell him everything but not tonight. Not on their first date.

"So, what is it you're retired from?" Lily asked, changing the subject.

He smiled contritely and pulled his hands from hers. "Sorry. I did it again."

Disappointment shot through her now that his hands were settled safely on his knees. She forced a smile. "I bet you were a businessman, right? Oh, wait, maybe a race-car driver or a lawyer," she added, throwing a finger in the air.

He erupted in laughter. "Wow! Businessman, race-car driver, lawyer? Why not all three?" He shook his head. "No, nothing as exciting as that. I was a stockbroker. Made a small fortune but hated the job, so I promised myself for my thirty-fifth birthday, I'd retire and move to a quaint little town to open up a business."

"A stockbroker?" Her mind drifted to Zander Lyons, the man her sister was seeing at the time of her murder. The majority owner of the largest brokerage house in New England. Zander, with his long, narrow face and pointy nose, was well into middle age without so much as one gray hair. It looked odd to Lily, that shaggy brown hair. So fake.

Sadness tugged at Lily's heart as she remembered the disagreement she'd had with Sara the day she was murdered.

"He's no good for you," Lily said. "You can do better." Her sister had blinders on when it came to that man.

"Honey, he's not as bad as you think," Sara said, then narrowed her eyes and tilted her head. "This isn't about Daddy and the money, is it? What he did to us—how he pitted us against each other all our lives, even from the grave? I know that's got to be bothering you. Is this where all the anger is coming from? 'Cause I'm more than willing…"

"No." Lily silenced her with a palm. "This has nothing to do with Daddy and the fact he left all his money to you, Sara." She took her sister's arm and linked hers through it, walking her over to the shade of a large maple tree. "As far as I'm concerned, I don't want one red cent of his money, *your* money. I'm perfectly happy with the diner, and I appreciate you signing it over to me. I know it doesn't hold the same sentimental value for you as it does for me." She looked earnestly into her sister's eyes. "I'm worried about you and what you've told me about Zander. He was really upset when he found out you were pregnant, remember?"

Her sister nodded, eyes downcast.

"And do you remember what he said?"

Sara's head shot up with those words. "He didn't mean it. He's just got a temper. It's his wife, you know, she causes him a lot of stress, and sometimes he lets his frustrations out on me."

"He told you he'd make sure one way or another that you'd lose the baby. He threatened the life of your child! Please, Sara, you're all I have left in this world, just you and the baby. We can't take any chances." She remembered the sudden surge of determination that gripped her at that moment. There was only one thing she could think of that would help Sara. "Just a sec, OK. I'll be right back." She left her sister and ran inside.

When she got back, Sara was sitting in her Lexus, engine running.

"Where're you going?" Lily asked as she approached the car.

"I've got some stuff to do."

Lily wasn't used to arguing with her sister, so she didn't know exactly what to say. Instead she put out her hand. She was holding a small-caliber pistol with a pearl handle. It had been their mother's. "Please take the gun. You probably won't need it, but I'd feel better knowing you have it."

Sara huffed and started to roll up the car window, but Lily pulled open the door. "Please."

"No," Sara yelled.

"I've got a feeling…a bad feeling. I know, sounds stupid, right? But I think you need this gun." She held her sister's gaze until, finally, Sara relented and took it, probably to appease Lily and no doubt just to be able to get the hell back home.

Lily pulled herself from her thoughts and back to Aiden. "Lucky for you to have so much freedom at such a young age," she said. Of course, she could have that kind of freedom too, if she wanted it. For now, she'd keep that bit of info to herself.

Aiden sipped his coffee. "Yeah. Guess I got lucky."

Their food arrived. When Elvira had refilled their cups and taken her leave, Aiden asked, "What about your parents? Do they live in Higgstown? Mine are in Chicago. Both retired and taking life easy."

And would there be a wife, ex-wife, or girlfriend you're not mentioning? Lily wondered as she forked the salad around her plate and fixed her meal with a concentrated stare. For the sake of the evening, she let the worry go.

She looked up from her food. "I'm afraid if we keep talking about my family you're going to bolt, and I'm looking forward to a lovely evening." She crunched on her salad. "How's your burger? Mashed potatoes any good?"

"Well, how 'bout I give them a try?" With a fork piled high, Aiden opened wide and shoveled them in. "Ummm, pretty good." He glanced at the wall clock over the cash register. "I suggest you start eatin', lovely lady. We're running out of time." His dimple came to life and her concerns melted away.

After dinner, instead of heading back to Aiden's truck, they walked a block and stopped in front of a historic three-story building. A brass plaque affixed beside the front door read "Dunnsville Town Hall, built 1897."

Soon a small crowd gathered beside them. "What's going on?" Lily asked, looking around at the growing group. There were couples, families, and a gang of noisy teens.

"Hope you're not scared of ghosts," Aiden whispered, taking her hand.

Again, the electric thrill of his touch raced up her arm. "Are we going on a ghost walk?"

Aiden nodded.

"How cool. I've always wanted to do that. What made you think of it?"

"With Halloween just weeks away, what could be more appropriate?" He moved closer and whispered in her ear, "Besides, I was thinking if it gets cold, we can cuddle up and I'll keep you warm." The heat of his breath on her neck turned her legs to rubber. She clutched his hand tighter and leaned against him.

They stood that way for a small forever. Not talking, just enjoying each other's company. When the crowd grew to a sufficient number, a man wearing a long black cape and holding a lantern came through the front door of the building. He stood on the top step, peering ominously down at the crowd. What was left of his frizzy, white, shoulder-length hair stuck out from under a beat-up top hat.

"Good evening, folks, and welcome to historic downtown Dunnsville." He stared out at the crowd with hooded eyes and a gruesome smile. "Follow me, if you dare." He let loose a cackle that brought gooseflesh to Lily's arms.

After a short lesson on the history of the town, the tour began, but Lily found it hard to concentrate. She could only focus on the man she was hanging onto. How ruggedly handsome he was, how tall and broad shouldered.

The tour was an hour and a half, but it flew by. They must have walked miles through the main streets of Dunnsville, and by the end of it, Aiden had wrapped an arm around her, pulling her in tight to warm her from the chilly night air.

"Do you believe in all this?" she asked as they walked, listening to the tales of hauntings of the old buildings that lined the downtown core of the small town.

"Believe what? What he's saying is true? That ghosts exist?" Aiden asked, a look of incredulousness on his face as if he was about to burst into laughter.

"Yeah."

"Are you kidding? It's just entertainment. There's no way what he's saying is true. Ghosts don't exist."

Lily flinched. "Where do you think we go when we die then?"

"Nowhere. Dead is dead. When we die, our bodies rot in the ground, and that's the end of us."

"I guess we all have our opinions." She forced a smile.

* * *

When they pulled into Lily's driveway, the inevitable sprang to mind. Should she invite him in for a drink or coffee? Would he kiss her? Butterflies sprang to life in her belly. For the most part, it had been a good date, relaxed and comfortable. Maybe it was best to keep it that way for now. Inviting him in for a nightcap might give the wrong impression. She smiled inwardly. Part of her wanted him to get that "wrong" impression.

"So," Aiden said, leaning in close once they got to her front door.

Her heart banged against her ribs. She knew he was going to kiss her. He didn't. Instead, Aiden gathered her in his arms and hugged her warmly. "I had a wonderful time tonight. Can I see you again?" he whispered into her hair.

"Yes. I'd like that," she said, trying to keep the disappointment from her voice. She'd wanted the kiss.

Aiden glanced at his watch. Lily sighed. Looked like the evening was over.

It was only 12:30. Aiden didn't want their date to end. "Then how 'bout right now?" he said with sudden inspiration.

An eyebrow raised into a question mark. "Whaddaya mean?"

Suddenly, he thought she might be thinking he was asking for sex in a roundabout way. "I mean this evening doesn't have to end. We could go somewhere for dessert.

We didn't have time for any at the diner." He spoke quickly, wanting to get the words out so she'd understand what he'd really meant.

A smile unfurled on Lily's lips. "I know just the place."

They soon found themselves sitting in what was fast becoming "their" booth—the middle one by the window. Lily hadn't turned on all the lights, just a couple in the back for some ambience.

"Be careful. It's hot," she warned as she placed a dish of steaming hot apple pie in front of Aiden. "Ice cream with that?"

"No thanks."

She poured each of them a cup of freshly brewed coffee and added a scoop of French vanilla to her own plate. The ice cream began to melt when it met the slab of pie.

"You know, you didn't have to do this. I feel bad." Aiden frowned. "I meant we could have gone somewhere other than *your* diner for dessert. Somewhere you didn't have to serve me."

Lily waved him off. "Ah, it's nothing; besides this is the only place in town to get dessert at this hour." She pulled the keys from her pocket and dangled them. "Higgstown Diner is open twenty-four hours a day for select customers only."

Aiden took a bite of his dessert. "Whoa, you're right. It is hot," he said around a mouthful of steaming apples.

"Fresh from the microwave."

He nodded and waved a hand in front of his open mouth in an attempt to cool the bite he'd taken.

"Shoulda had some ice cream, cools it down quicker." Lily stood, looking a little concerned.

He covered his mouth with a napkin, a little embarrassed. She left him for a moment and returned with a glass of ice water.

Way to give a great impression, tough guy, he chided himself. The skin on the roof of his mouth had blistered. He finally got the pie down with the aid of the water. "Thanks."

"It's my fault. Guess I had the pie in the microwave a touch too long." She splayed a hand over her chest and looked genuinely concerned. "You OK now?"

He nodded. His eyes were drawn to those long, tapered fingers and her breasts. God, she was sexy. His mind flitted to how much he wished she would touch him with those hands. Run them through his hair, across his bare chest...

"So, where are you staying?" Lily asked.

"I'm renting a log cabin just a few minutes outside town, on Ryan's Road. Basically in the middle of nowhere."

"Yeah, I know the place. It's beautiful, but it's pretty deserted up there. Old man Hutchinson built it for his son, Ryan, a few years back. It's been empty for a while."

"Ah, hence the name 'Ryan's Road'." Aiden grinned. "Why isn't Ryan living in it?"

"He was killed in Afghanistan. His father passed away shortly after. Everyone says he died of a broken heart."

Aiden gave his head a solemn shake. "Damn shame. What about his mother?"

Lily looked thoughtful. "You know, I don't know anything about her. Never met the woman. I think they'd divorced when Ryan was just a boy."

"Wow, that's a sad story. Who owns it now?"

"One of Hutchinsons' nephews, I think. He usually rents it out to the summer people. I've never seen the inside, but it looks gorgeous from the outside." Lily's brows knitted in contemplation. "How come you didn't know that? I mean you rented the place."

"Oh, I didn't ask any questions about the history of the cabin. I just called a real estate agent before coming out here. He'd sent some pictures and that was enough for me," he lied, then forked up another piece of pie, but blew on it heartily before letting it pass through his lips. "Would you like to come see it tomorrow?"

After a moment's hesitation, she nodded. "Sure."

"Great! What time do you get off work?"

"It's my day off, but I've got a few errands. Every Thursday morning I go to the Evelyn Harrison Seniors Center and visit with a few...friends."

"I don't have much planned. What time would you like me to come get you?" Aiden asked.

"Don't worry about picking me up. I know where the cabin is. How about I come up around four? I can bring some groceries and make us dinner."

Aiden held up a hand. "No way. You can drive up on your own, but I'll make dinner." He did a mental scan of his cupboards and fridge. There wasn't much except junk food and beer. Looks like grocery shopping would be on his to-do list. But what would he cook? The only dish he knew was spaghetti and meatballs. "Hope you like Italian."

Lily leaned back in her seat, looking content. "Wow, a man who can cook." She smiled. "I love Italian. Can't wait. Can I bring anything?"

Nothing, he thought, except that sexy little body. And all your secrets of course.

A sly grin unfurled on his lips. "No. Just you, Lily…" Aiden stopped himself just in time. He'd almost said her last name. "You know, I don't even know your last name."

"Geez, you're right." She tilted her head and took him in. "It feels like I've known you forever. I keep forgetting we've only just met. It's Valier. My father was French Canadian."

Here was his opportunity. He knew a little about her family from what the sheriff had told him, but Wilkins had warned him Lily was notoriously private. *A hard nut to crack,* were his exact words.

"Tell me about your dad. What kind of man is he? What does he do for a living? Or is he retired?" Aiden feigned ignorance. Starting in about dear old dad would be a good segue into the whole sibling rivalry. He couldn't imagine a father leaving his fortune to only one of his children. That had to have pushed a few of Lily's buttons.

She smiled, but it was without humor. "Let's talk about something more interesting, like when you're going to start looking for that little business you want to open. Maybe I can help."

Wilkins was right. Lily Valier was a hard nut to crack. How many more times could he risk bringing up her family before she became suspicious?

Aiden got to his feet and took Lily's hands, tugging her up with him. "Maybe we shouldn't talk at all." He pulled her in close, wrapped an arm tightly around her waist, and lowered his mouth to hers. The feel of her soft lips on his stirred him. She let out a low moan, and her hands were suddenly in his hair, pulling him hungrily toward her.

Outside, snowflakes fell, twinkling in the streetlights.

CHAPTER 5

Lily lay in bed, staring at the ceiling. The excitement of her date and the dull ache of yearning kept her from settling into slumber. She relived their kiss over and over again. Still, in her imagination she felt the warmth of Aiden's lips and the gentle strength of his hands on her body. Shock waves of desire rippled through her, and she wished more than anything he were here beside her now. Finally, sometime in the wee hours, sleep took her in gentle hands.

Lily woke the same way she fell asleep, with Aiden on her mind. For the first time in a long time, she was looking forward to her day.

She waited for the morning crowd to thin before stopping by the diner. A cup of much-needed coffee and something to eat wasn't all she wanted. Since Sara's death, friends had dropped out of her life as quickly and as thoroughly as if she had bubonic plague, and she yearned for some girl talk, especially now.

Lily settled at the counter. Annie, who was working the grill, turned to greet her. "Hey, whatcha doin' here on your day off?"

"I'm just a regular customer today, Annie." Lily turned over the cup in front of her. "A nice cuppa coffee and a piece of toast and jam is all I ask." She smiled.

"Comin' right up." Annie poured each of them a coffee and was back in a flash with the toast and jam.

"How was the breakfast crowd?" Lily asked.

"Oh, about the same as usual. Good turnout." Annie gestured with a nod of her head to the window. "Can you believe it? Snow this early in the season?"

True, Lily had thought it odd the snow had started so early, but her mood was so upbeat a hurricane could blow through town and she wouldn't care.

She shrugged and smiled. "Weird, I know, but it's not like it hasn't *ever* snowed in October before."

Annie's eyes suddenly narrowed as she leaned on the counter, taking Lily in. "Why the goofy grin?"

Although Annie was an employee, there was a spark of friendship between them. "I don't know what you're talking about?" Lily replied with a wink.

"Ya got a funny-lookin' smile on your face. What's going on? Spill." Annie rested her head in her hands. Hair pulled back in a ponytail, she looked younger than her forty-five years.

Lily sipped her coffee. "I've met someone."

Annie squealed. "Oh, and I bet I know who it is." She clapped her hands. "That gorgeous hunk of a man who was in here yesterday. Am I right?"

Lily nodded, happy to have someone to share her joy with.

"And he's the one who saved you the other night, too. By God, Lil, things happen for a reason. If the place wasn't being robbed, and he hadn't come by just then to help you, you never would have met and…"

Lily stilled her with a hand. "Must be divine intervention." She smirked.

"Damn right. The Lord knows what we want and what we need, and He sends it to us when the time is right." Annie fingered the tiny gold cross around her neck.

Lily liked that thought, but although she wanted to, she couldn't accept it. If Aiden was sent to her by God, then why didn't God save her sister and the baby growing inside her? It would have been beyond wonderful to have a niece or nephew, to build a family again after her mom's passing last year. She pushed the thoughts away, not wanting them to crowd out the happy ones she'd started her day with.

"He took me out last night," Lily continued.

Annie's eyes widened. "Oh, do tell. And I want *all* the details."

Lily leisurely spread strawberry jam on her toast, teasing her friend by taking her time in replying.

"Aw, come on. You know I have no life. Just a few small details," Annie pleaded.

Lily laughed heartily and it felt good. "There's not much to tell, really. He took me on a ghost walk in Dunnsville. That's all."

"Oooohhh, that sounds nice and cozy. Did ya get a kiss at the end of the evening or a little something more?" Annie winked.

Lily's eyes strayed to the spot in the diner where Aiden had kissed her. "Maybe." She took a bite of toast.

Annie clapped her hands again. "You go, girl! You two going out on another date?"

"I'm going to see the place where he's staying later this afternoon. You know that log cabin on Ryan's Road?"

"Oh, sure. Everybody knows that place. He gonna be around for a while?"

Lily smiled. "Looks that way." She drained her coffee and finished off the toast.

Annie placed a hand on Lily's. "I'm happy for ya. After all you've been through with losing your sister and mother, you deserve some happiness."

Lily was genuinely touched. Annie's words felt sincere. "Thanks, Annie. You might be the only one in town who thinks I deserve anything except a nice cozy jail cell."

Her friend waved a hand in the air. "Don't let these closed-minded small-town folk get the better of ya. People are gonna talk no matter what." Annie's expression darkened and she leaned in close. "Does this new fella know about..." Her words trailed off and she began again, "Does he know about the money and all that?"

Lily was surprised Annie broached the subject. Perhaps she was feeling a little more like a friend than an employee. Maybe that wasn't such a bad thing. Still, the wall of protection she'd built up around herself after her sister's murder was hard to get around. She'd confided in Annie, but she'd certainly not told her everything.

Annie shifted uncomfortably. "I spoke out of turn. I'm sorry."

"No"—Lily was quick to answer—"it's OK. Aiden knows about my sister's death, but that's it. He has no idea about my inheritance or that I'm a suspect in Sara's murder." She sighed. "I suppose I'll have to tell him or he'll find out on his own. But I'm scared he'll bolt."

"My advice is to just have fun for now. You'll know when the time is right to tell him more, and besides, once he gets to know you, he'll figure out for himself you're a good woman."

Lily wondered if Annie was right. After all, the townsfolk did have good reason for feeling the way they did. If she put herself in their shoes, their suspicions were understandable, especially because of the argument she'd had with Sara the day of her murder, and, of course, there was that damned e-mail. Information spread quicker than a cold in January in small towns like Higgstown.

Lily glanced at her watch. "Gotta go, Annie. Thanks for listening."

"Where you off to?"

Lily threw her purse over a shoulder. "Three guesses."

* * *

Visiting the residents of the Evelyn Harrison Seniors Center was bittersweet for Lily. The bright fluorescents made her eyes tired, and the harsh antiseptic smell was one she'd never get used to. It nearly stole her breath every time she walked through the front doors into the pea-green atrium. She stamped her feet free of snow as she made her way to the reception area.

"Hey, Miss Lily, nice to see you today." Gail, a rail-thin black woman in her fifties, greeted Lily from her post. "How 'bout that weather?" She shook her head in disbelief.

"I know! It's a little unexpected. Haven't even dug my boots out yet." Her toes were wet and chilled in her Sketchers. "Is everyone behaving themselves today? No wild parties?"

Gail laughed. "Things are quiet, but I imagine once they see you're here, it'll liven up pretty quick. Need any help?" She gestured to the buggy filled to overflowing that Lily had wheeled in behind her.

"Got it covered, but thanks. I'll just start on my rounds if that's OK."

"Sure, honey, you go right ahead."

Lily had been visiting the residents of the center since she was a teenager. It was something she was compelled to do, more than likely because she'd never had a grandparent of her own. Both sets on her mother's and father's sides died when she was just a girl, and she had no memories of what it felt like to have an older person in her life.

Over the years, the faces of the elderly residents came and went. Some were in Lily's life for years and others just months, but she remembered most of them. The women in the facility outnumbered the men two to one, and the old fellas were often fought over by the ladies. It was comical how they would argue and fuss over them as if they were their husbands. Lily suspected the men secretly enjoyed the attention, though they grumbled and complained and would never admit to it.

She made her way to the common room where the majority of the residents would be watching the big-screen TV she'd bought for the center last month. Others would be playing cards or sitting around chatting.

The room was large and open. Picture windows made up an entire wall, letting in natural light, softening the artificial fluorescents. Laminate, yellowed with age and scarred with scrapes from wheelchairs, walkers, and canes covered the floor; the painted brick walls were cold and institutional-looking, though one was dressed up with a hand-painted mural of a flower-filled meadow, complete with rainbows and butterflies. A bit juvenile, Lily thought, but in fairness, it had been done by art students from Higgstown High.

She entered, pulling her buggy, and waved and smiled at the familiar faces.

"My goodness, is that Lily?" she heard someone ask in a voice shaky with age. It was Irene Scott—ninety-two with failing eyesight, but she always seemed to know Lily when she arrived.

"Yes, Mrs. Scott, it's me," Lily called back loudly and took a seat on one of the couches. Soon her friends were settling in around her.

"Is it visiting day already?" Mr. Piccione asked as he approached with his walker. A portly man with a tidy, thin mustache, he was never without his fedora and sports coat, making him look as if he'd walked straight out of a 1950s gangster movie.

"Don't you even know what day it is?" one of the ladies called.

Mr. Piccione shot her a dirty look and settled beside Lily. "How's my girl today?" He patted her knee with an age-speckled hand.

"Just great, Mr. P." She gave him her warmest smile. "I have something for you all."

"What? What did you say?" Mrs. Scott called. Her hearing was about as good as her eyesight.

"She said she has something for us." Mr. Piccione spoke loudly, enunciating each word, then returned his gaze to Lily. "You're such a sweetie. You *always* have something for us."

An air of excitement filled the room. The nurses and attendants sat back and let Lily have center stage. "I brought some large-print novels as well as books on tape, and I have a few treats, but of course I've got to let the staff take care of those because some of you are on restricted diets."

"Not me, angel," came a call from the back. Lily turned to see Mrs. Guiterrez smiling at her. Mrs. G., as Lily called her, was a little thing with jet-black hair. It was the kind that came from a bottle and was startling against the pale of her wrinkled face. She held a special place in Lily's heart and had lived in the center for as long as Lily could remember.

Lily waved her over. "Good for you, Mrs. G. You keep doing whatever it is you're doing to stay so healthy."

The old woman walked briskly and confidently over to the couch and perched on the armrest beside Lily, wrapping an arm around her as if to lay claim. Mrs. G. had no children, and her husband had passed away long ago. Though she had some extended family, nieces and nephews who visited from time to time, Lily and her friends at the center had become as close as family. Lily suspected it was the sense of being alone in the world that had brought the two of them even closer over the last little while.

"Love you, angel," Mrs. G. whispered, and Lily smiled up at her, giving her a wink. It might have made the others feel bad if Lily had said, "I love you, too," but the wink let her friend know she did.

Lily continued unloading the buggy. "I've got wool and patterns for the ladies and crossword and Sudoku puzzles, as well as some paint by numbers. We'll set them out on the table at the back, and you can take whatever you like."

Sharon, a long-time employee who was so ancient she could easily pass for a resident, shuffled over and scooped up the goodies Lily had unpacked. "I'll take the treats to the kitchen. We'll sort out who can have what later."

"Thanks," Lily replied. "I brought some sugarless treats, too."

"You always do," Sharon called over her shoulder.

After a half hour of chatting in the common room, Lily visited some of the bedridden residents and the ones who preferred the solitude of their rooms to the common areas. She spent a good amount of time with each, never rushing and always patient, even with those who tried to keep her with them, not wanting to let go of the company. She left a present with each of them—a book, a DVD, a jigsaw puzzle. After so many years, she never grew tired of the weekly visits, and now that she had money, she was all too happy to buy a big-ticket item for the facility every now and then. After all, she had more than she could spend in a lifetime and her needs were simple.

When she was done, she went back to the common room and bade a quick good-bye from the doorway. She was met with waves, blowing of kisses, smiles, and thank-yous.

Leaving was always sad. She couldn't help but wonder if everyone would still be there next week when she returned. Life was a precarious thing at any age.

On her way to the car, her cell phone rang. The sight of Aiden's name on the phone made her heartbeat quicken.

She let it ring one more time then answered, trying not to seem too eager.

"Hi. I was just thinking about you and wanted to hear your voice. Where are you?" Aiden said.

Lily's heart did a flip-flop. He was thinking of her! "Just running a few errands. I'll be heading home soon."

"Does it always snow here in October?" He laughed. "I wasn't prepared for this."

"No. This is just weird. I'm getting into my car now, and it's really coming down. I've got on a warm enough coat, but no boots. My feet are soaked." She hoped the premature winter weather wouldn't make him second-guess his move to small-town Maine.

"Hope it doesn't pile up. You might have a hard time getting up my driveway. It's pretty steep."

Disappointment struck. Was he going to cancel on her? "It should be fine," she said, but worry stabbed when she realized she didn't have her snow tires on yet.

"OK. You know this town better than I do. If you still want to come to the cabin, it's more than fine with me."

She heard the smile in his voice and that made her relax. "No worries. I'll be there at four."

CHAPTER 6

Aiden yanked on the bill of his cap so that it concealed much of his face, then threw on the hood of his fleece jacket as an added protection. Lily was on her way home. That was good. There'd be no chance he'd run into her on his way to see Sheriff Wilkins.

There were others who might recognize him and rat him out to Lily. He was thinking of the regulars at the diner. As the stranger in town, he'd noticed their curious stares and heard the whispered questions. There was Annie too. It hadn't been suspicion in her eyes, but something far worse, *attraction*. He didn't think she'd make a play for him, but she might be on the lookout, hoping they'd run into each other.

Snow fell in heavy wet dollops. What a godforsaken place. Snow in bloody October! He'd stuffed his folder on the Valier case safely inside his jacket to keep it from getting soaked.

Parking spots were hard to come by on the short strip of the downtown core, but he'd found one up the street from the sheriff's department and had to hoof it through the sloppy white stuff. Good packing snow, he thought absurdly. Maybe building a snowman would be in his future.

As he walked along the double-wide sidewalk, he couldn't imagine Higgstown in its midsummer glory, all bright and sunny, filled to brimming with tourists. This day was gray and cold. The kind that chilled to the bone. He stuck close to the storefronts. Most were canopied and kept the snow off him. His fleece jacket soaked up the flakes as well as any sponge would. As he walked, he glanced into the stores and made mental notes. The menswear shop had a warm-looking jacket in the window. He'd stop in on his way back.

He spied an A&P. Spaghetti and meatballs, he reminded himself.

He came to the small, unassuming red-bricked police station on the corner of King and Elm Streets. Next to it stood a furniture store and across the street, a coffee shop and real estate office.

Aiden remembered the first time he met with Wilkins and how he'd thought of Lily Valier simply as a murderer who'd, so far, managed not to get caught. He was surprised at how, in just a few short days, a crack had opened as to the possibility of her innocence. Usually his instincts kicked in and he knew in an instant whether someone was guilty or not, and ninety-nine percent of the time, they were. He couldn't get over the feeling he knew Lily. *Really* knew her. And when they'd kissed, he felt something, something more than desire. Holding her in his arms felt way too comfortable for a man being paid to sweep her off her feet. A niggling of guilt sneaked up on him.

Antonio met Aiden at the front desk. The sour-faced deputy lifted his head from his paperwork and gave a little nod. His wispy moustache twitched up in a short but quickly fading smile.

"Hey, Antonio."

"He's in his office," Antonio said, his tone curt.

Aiden knew the way. It would be damned near impossible to get lost in the small building. A few strides down the hallway brought him to the sheriff's door.

Wilkins checked his watch. "Right on time."

Aiden smiled. "Of course. I'm nothing if not reliable."

"Sit." Wilkins gestured to the battered, institutional-looking chair in front of his desk. "Coffee?"

"No, I'm good." Aiden removed his cap and tossed it onto another ancient chair, along with his damp jacket.

The office was sparse. Wilkins's desk, circa 1960, was a clunker of dull gray metal. On its surface lay an ink-stained blotter. Framed family pictures populated a corner, and on the other side stood a half-inch stack of papers.

Sleepy town with not much going on. His days must sloth by like the proverbial molasses in January. The Sara Valier murder was surely the most exciting thing to hit this place in like...forever. It was no wonder Aiden had been called in. Every time he looked into Wilkins's eyes, he saw his desperation to put the case to rest.

Aiden placed his folder on the desk in front of him and took a seat. After rubbing the circulation back into his hands, he flipped it open.

"Before we get started, let me call Deluca in here." The sheriff punched in an extension number on his desk phone and a moment later, Antonio sauntered in.

Aiden moved to take his stuff off the chair beside him to make room for the deputy to sit.

"Leave it," Deluca said. "I'll stand." He crossed his arms and leaned against the wall.

"Got anything yet?" Wilkins asked Aiden.

Aiden sucked in a breath and let it out in a huff. "Like you said, Lily Valier's a hard nut to crack."

"Nothin'?" The sheriff sighed and leaned back, his tired old chair squalling in protest.

Aiden gave Wilkins his best smile. "I'm seeing her again tonight, and I think she likes me. No worries, sheriff, Lily *will* let her guard down. But, in the meantime, I've got some questions."

Everything had seemed so cut and dried when he and the sheriff first spoke. Lily Valier was guilty of her sister's murder and that was that. Both the sheriff and his deputy were sure of it. All Aiden had to do was charm her with his wits and good looks and she'd melt. He'd be out of town in no time with seven grand to add to his bank account.

He looked again at the horrible pictures of Lily. True despair was in that face. Surely he could tell the difference between despair and guilt? With a sigh, Aiden flipped the photos over and pulled out the list of questions he'd jotted down that morning.

"Tell me about Zander Lyons."

The sheriff crossed his arms and took a breath. "Well, he admitted to fathering Sara Valier's baby. They'd had an affair that lasted a little over a year, and he's a married man with a grown daughter. Think she's nineteen or twenty." His tone was matter-of-fact.

"He didn't kill her," Deluca said.

Aiden turned to him. "And you know this, how? I can't imagine he was thrilled when he knocked up his mistress."

Deluca gave Aiden the once-over as if sizing him up. His lips thinned into a line of displeasure. "He's not our guy."

Aiden had to fight the urge to stand up. He was twice the size of Deluca and wanted to let the man know he wasn't easily intimidated, but he kept his mouth shut, not willing to bite the hand that feeds and all that crap.

Wilkins was no picnic to deal with, but at least he made an attempt at hiding his distaste in dealing with an outsider. However, Deluca's displeasure at Aiden nosing around the investigation was very much apparent.

"He's rich and has a high profile in the community. Think of what this scandal would do to him," Aiden said to Deluca, an edge to his voice.

Deluca raised a brow. "His alibi is as tight as spandex over a fat chick's ass. He was out of the country when Miss Valier was killed. Checked it out myself and it's airtight."

The deputy could be Zander Lyon's lawyer with the way he was defending him. Aiden grew tense, muscles tightening, jaw grinding. He cracked and popped the tension away with a side-to-side twist of his head. "He could have hired someone."

The sheriff leaned forward. "We thought of that. There's no evidence pointing to a murder-for-hire scheme." He sighed and shook his head. "As much as I hate to admit it, facts are facts and what we've got on Lily, although circumstantial *at the moment*, is enough for me to think she did it."

Deluca chimed in, "You never really know what someone is capable of. When I worked homicide in Bangor, there were plenty of people as *nice* as Lily who did very bad things. Mostly heat-of-the-moment stuff, but that doesn't make them any less guilty." He put his hands on the back of the chair beside Aiden and leaned forward. "Lily was seen holding a gun on her sister. Remember the e-mail from Sara Valier's ex-boyfriend? He saw her with the gun." He said the last few words slowly, driving home his point.

Aiden knew about the gun and the e-mail, but realized it would take some time before Lily would tell him that story, if ever. What reason would she have to hold a gun on her sister? Did Lily want her half of the money? She didn't seem the money hungry type, living simply, still working seemingly because she wanted to. It just didn't make sense. Nevertheless, a small knot of concern began to grow, supported by the fact the weapon had never been found.

"An e-mail from a stalker ex-boyfriend is hardly proof," Aiden argued.

"Philip wasn't *stalking* Sara." Wilkins gave a small laugh. "He was hurt after she left him for Zander and drove by Lily's place looking for Sara so they could talk. I know Phil. He's a mild-mannered, sweet guy."

"That would be *my* definition of stalking," Aiden replied. "Was Philip Kemp cleared of the murder too?" Aiden narrowed his gaze and studied Wilkins.

"I questioned Phil. No way he did it," Wilkins said.

"Mind if I pay him a visit?" Aiden asked.

"Knock yourself out." Deluca pulled a beaten-up business card from his shirt pocket and tossed it to Aiden. "He runs a garage here in town. Hell of a mechanic."

Aiden took the card and placed it in the folder before closing it. He looked at each man; he had to ask the question burning a hole in his gut. "Why are you two so dead set on nailing Lily for this crime? Do you really think she has it in her to kill her pregnant sister?"

"Look, ya know the facts by now. Sara was shot with a small-caliber weapon, we have a witness who says he saw Lily pointing a gun at Sara…and…" Deluca wagged a finger. "She's got one hell of a motive to want her sister dead. Lily Valier's a very rich woman now."

"Their dad was a sick bastard, always pitting them girls against each other. Sara was his favorite, and when he died, he left every penny to her and Lily got zilch. I think that would be enough to make her just a little angry," Wilkins added.

Aiden tapped a finger to his lips. He knew about dear old dad and his games—it didn't seem enough. Besides, there was still one big unknown. "Do you know if Sara was willing to share the wealth with her sister?"

Wilkins and Deluca eyed each other, then Deluca answered, "Their dad, Jack Valier, died eight months ago. Don't you think in that time, if Sara was going to give Lily half the estate, she would have done it? We checked, Mr. O'Rourke, and there were no lump-sum payments made to Lily Valier before her sister's death. So the answer to your question is no, Sara did not share her inheritance with her sister."

"But you didn't come right out and ask Lily about the money?" Aiden said.

Deluca rolled his eyes. "Like I said earlier, Mr. O'Rourke, I worked up in Bangor for a few years, in homicide, so I know what I'm doing. Got plenty of experience handling these types of cases. We didn't have to ask Miss Valier about the money. Unless she's stuffed it under her mattress, she doesn't have it. We checked her bank accounts. That's proof enough."

Why the hell did you hire me then? Aiden wanted to ask, but he knew it was Wilkins's idea to bring him in on the investigation—probably driven to it by desperation. Aiden decided to change tack. No use arguing with Deluca, the knucklehead. "So, this Philip guy, he saw Lily holding a gun on Sara in front of Lily's house, right?"

The sheriff nodded.

"Well, Sara wasn't shot on Lily's property. She was found dead in her own house." He held up a stilling hand when the sheriff opened his mouth to reply. "I know what you're going to say. Lily went home with Sara and shot her there. But it doesn't make sense that Philip would just sit idly by and let that happen. Why didn't he do something? Follow them or at least call the cops if he thought the woman he loved was in danger."

Wilkins threw his hands in the air in a gesture of surrender. "Guess everyone reacts differently in an emergency. Some bolt, some help. Could be Phil's way of helping was to send that e-mail."

Aiden stood and gathered his things. "Thanks. I'll be in touch." He could use a set of snows on his pickup, and he knew just the place to get them.

As he stepped outside, a tingle ran down his spine, giving him the feeling he was being watched. He looked around furtively, replacing his cap and making sure to pull the hood of his soaked jacket over his head. He spotted no one but just couldn't shake his unease as he made his way to that menswear shop. A nice waterproof jacket was certainly in order.

CHAPTER 7

Before going home to get ready for her dinner with Aiden, Lily stopped by the diner. There was a vintage Merlot tucked away somewhere in the back. The staff at the seniors center had given it to her as a thank-you for the TV, but knowing how expensive it was, she couldn't bring herself to open it without a special occasion to celebrate. Silly, she knew, since she could buy a whole case if she wanted, but New England practicality was in her bones.

She decided to enter the restaurant through the back door, grab the vino, and get home so she could make herself pretty. That thought stopped her cold. Since when did Lily Valier care about making herself pretty for a man? She couldn't help but laugh. Since the day Aiden rolled into town, she reminded herself.

He could leave just as easily.

Worry knotted her belly, but she pushed the thought away. No, she wouldn't let negativity kill the potential for happiness, and what's more, after giving it some thought, she'd decided to be more open with Aiden despite Annie's advice to take it slow. If he asked questions, she'd do her best to answer them. If he was really going to stay in town, it would be near impossible to keep secrets from him anyway. Like ripping a bandage from a wound, a part of her wanted to get it over with—no use dragging things out and risking falling in love, only to have him leave when the skeletons in her closet came tumbling out.

Lily went to her office and looked around, trying to remember where she'd stored the wine. A wave of nostalgia hit her. It had been happening a lot since her sister's death. It was if she was looking at the place with new eyes.

If was hard to believe she'd actually lived in the diner with her mother and sister for several years when they first moved to town. Her office used to be their bedroom. She smiled as she recalled how all three of them shared the double bed. How cozy it had been, how safe and fun. The staff room across the hall was their family room, where many nights were spent watching television together. The small storage room had been a den of sorts, where she and Sara sat side by side at a small desk, doing their homework.

She walked over to the couch and looked at the photos on the wall above it. All in identical black wooden frames, they were a tribute to the Valier women, spanning the years. Every picture was of either Sara, herself, or their mother and sometimes the three of them together. Smiling faces and interlocked arms showed the world how happy they'd been.

Now, through a cruel twist of fate, she was the last one standing. Lily kissed her fingertip and planted the gesture of affection on a picture of her mother, and then on one of Sara. "Love you guys," she said.

Tears burned her eyes, but to staunch them, she searched deep down inside herself for something to be grateful about. Lily thought of the diner. Not the greatest prize in the world, but it was one she wouldn't trade...*couldn't* trade, unless she was willing to give over her heart and soul in the bargain. This place held her memories and kept alive the spirit of the people who meant the most to her.

With a sigh, Lily sat on her desk chair, looked down, and spied the wine tucked away, still in the decorative little pine box the staff had presented it to her in. She reached down and grabbed it, blew the dust off, and went home to get ready.

* * *

A few hours later, Lily was sailing her way along the narrow, snow-slicked driveway up to Aiden's cabin. If one could even call the swath of mowed-down forest a driveway. It was more like a trail tamped down by the continued passage of cars and feet. There were light posts every so often and for that she was grateful.

"What the hell am I doing?" she said out loud. "This is nuts." There was still enough sunlight to see the driveway, but later she'd be on her way back down in the dark *and* without her snows on. Was she truly so blinded by this handsome stranger that she was willing to not only take her life in her hands, but also chance being stranded with him?

Lily glanced in her rear-view mirror. The driveway was too narrow to make a three-point turn, and there was no way she could back out all the way to the road. So she continued cautiously to the cabin that was slowly growing larger as she neared.

Large, wet flakes splatted on her windshield, and between swipes of the wiper blades, she spied Aiden, shovel in hand, clearing what he could. The stairs to the front porch were free of the white stuff as was a patch of driveway about twenty feet by twenty feet. He looked up with a smile when he saw the flicker of headlights.

She crunched to a stop just a few feet from him, grabbed her purse and the wine, and got out of the car.

He leaned the shovel against the porch railing. "God, I'm so sorry to make you drive here. I should have picked you up."

"No worries. It was a piece of cake," she lied as she pressed the lock button on her key fob.

Aiden grinned. "Did you really just do that?"

"Do what?"

"You do realize we're in the wilderness here. What do you think, a bear or coyote's gonna jack your car?"

She handed the wine over. "One can never be too careful."

"You know, I haven't even locked the front door once." He laughed, then, spying the pine box housing the Merlot, he said, "I told you not to bring anything."

She threw him a wink as she made her way up the stairs toward the front door. "Nice jacket."

The cabin was smaller than it looked from the outside. From the road below, it seemed to loom large from its place on the hill, like a sentinel, keeping watch over passersby. The cabin was constructed of pine logs with an A-line sloping roof and huge picture windows. Its high vaulted ceilings and even larger windows, which ran across the entire back of the cabin, gave it an open, spacious feel. The heavenly scent of pine surrounded Lily and she took it in, savoring a few deep breaths.

Aiden took her jacket to hang in the closet. "Please, go make yourself comfortable." He gestured toward the living room straight ahead of them. "I'll build a fire."

Two rich brown leather sofas were set in a large L in front of a granite fireplace that went from floor to vaulted ceiling. As Lily spun in a slow circle taking in the place, she spotted a loft over the back of the living room. His bedroom. She wondered if she would be seeing it tonight. The prospect of warming Aiden's bed brought on a lustful longing.

The fire sounded like a great idea—a little cliché maybe, but she supposed it was what people did in log cabins. No bearskin rug in front of the fireplace, but there was a cozy-looking area rug. She stifled a smile. Her imagination was starting to run away with her again.

"Be right back." Aiden walked to the kitchen at the front of the cabin, adjacent to the living room. There was barely a wall in sight. Only the occasional sturdy wooden pillar stood in place, holding up the structure.

Lily sank into the soft leather sofa, curled her legs up under her, and covered herself with the fluffy throw draped over the arm of the couch. Gooseflesh pricked her arms, but she'd soon be warmed by a fire and wine and perhaps even by Aiden.

He came back carrying a tray with an assortment of cheese, crackers, and pâté. After setting it down on the coffee table, he gave her a quick smile and was gone again. This time when he returned, he had the wine she'd brought and two plastic glasses.

"Here you go." He handed over a half-filled glass of plum-colored liquid. "Sorry for the plastic. I should have bought some real wineglasses. Wasn't thinking." Then he poured some for himself. "A toast." Aiden held his up and Lily did the same. "To the most beautiful woman in town." They touched rims and sipped.

His gaze lingered and she felt herself flush, but not enough to turn away. It was damn good to have a man look at her the way he did. Those hungry eyes made her feel sexy. Lily let her own gaze roam down to his checkered flannel shirt. He looked like he belonged in the Maine wilderness. The top two snaps were undone, giving her a glimpse of a well-muscled chest. She toyed with the idea of reaching out and tugging open the rest of the snaps on that shirt.

"You look like you're thinking something wicked." He raised a questioning brow.

Lily took another sip of Merlot, a coy little smile playing on her lips. "Maybe I am."

"Tell me then. What wicked thoughts could possibly be going through that pretty head of yours?"

She reached for some cheese and a couple of crackers. "Maybe later," she said, leaning back into the softness of the sofa, the Merlot already beginning to work its magic.

Aiden stretched an arm across the back of the couch, his fingers finding her hair. "I'll know your secrets sooner or later," he teased as he trailed a finger up her neck and along her jawline.

If he kept this up, he just might.

He put his glass down and stood suddenly. "Can't believe I forgot the fire." He chuckled as he made his way to the hearth.

Never mind that, get back here and touch me again, Lily wanted to say, but all she managed was a smile.

"So, how long have you lived in Higgstown?" he asked over his shoulder while piling kindling and crumpled newspaper into a mound.

"Since I was seven. Mom moved Sara and me here after my parents divorced."

"I'm sorry to hear that. I mean about the divorce. It must have been hard on you and your sister."

"It was. At least at first, but we found comfort in each other." She thought about those days. Their dad had been a troubled man who took out his frustrations on Lily and their mother. Sara learned at an early age how to manage him and always slipped under his radar.

Aiden turned toward her, a log in each hand. "You don't talk about your family much. Is there a reason for that?" He looked genuinely concerned and that melted her heart a little.

She drained her wineglass, poured some more, and decided to answer. "Dad was"—she wanted to say "an asshole" but softened her language—"an abusive man. Mom put up with his crap way too long. It took her a while to find the strength and resources to leave him. We didn't have much and what little we did have, Dad lost gambling. It's a miracle we finally got away."

"At least you did in the end. That's what counts."

Lily's throat cinched. Should she tell him more about her parents? That they were dead? Aiden had a way of making her feel safe, as if she could say anything and he would support her, even comfort her. The wine had melted her defenses. Perhaps it wouldn't be so bad to give him a few more personal details. "My parents are both deceased. Dad died when his plane crashed while landing on his way back from New York City. A stroke killed my mother."

"Sorry to hear that." There was sympathy in his voice, but she could see in his eyes that the words "plane crash" had piqued his interest. "You don't hear of people dying in plane crashes very often. Was it a commercial flight? Sounds like a huge tragedy."

Lily reached for her wine; a few more sips were in order. "Private plane. Just Dad and the pilot on board."

Aiden's eyes grew wide. "That's something you hear even less often."

Lily nodded her reply. The big kick in the ass was that her dad made his money after the divorce, leaving their mother to continue struggling. There were never support payments, and too many years had passed after they'd divided up their meager assets for her mom to go after him. At least that's what her mom had said, but deep down, Lily thought she just didn't want anything to do with him ever again and decided to let sleeping dogs lie.

The fire was blazing now, and Aiden took a seat beside her on the sofa. "I guess it's safe to say he was a wealthy man?" He topped up her glass and sipped from his own.

"A millionaire many times over. Fell in with the right business partners. He wasn't the smartest guy, but he could charm acorns from a squirrel." Lily felt the inevitable coming. The next question would be: where was the money now? Then Aiden O'Rourke would be like all the rest of the men she'd dated. She'd tell him how her father left his fortune to Sara, and only Sara, and how she'd inherited it after her sister's death. Was it wrong to tell him so much so soon? She sidled away and nibbled on more crackers and cheese.

"Ever feel like leaving town?" His question surprised her.

Where was *the* question? She tried not to look surprised. "No. This is my home."

"But Higgstown is so small; everyone must know your business."

She nodded. "True. There are no secrets in this town." There was something strangely comforting in knowing what people thought about you. Would it be easier in a city? In a place where she could blend into the crowd and be anonymous? Maybe, but here her roots ran deep and firm, and it would take a hell of a lot to run her out of her own town.

"And what secrets do you have?" He grinned.

She shifted her gaze, tentative and uncertain. Was he teasing her? "Well…" She drained her glass. "Um…" Why was she so nervous? Everyone had secrets, but what innocuous thing could she say that would throw him off this subject, maybe even coax a smile?

Aiden took her hand. "Are you OK? I was just kidding around."

She forced a smile but couldn't help wonder if she should test the waters, give him what he wanted. It was unlike her to open up so quickly and easily, but his touch made her yearn to trust him. The words came out before she had the chance to think it through. "My secrets might change your opinion of me. You sure you want to hear them?"

He let go of her hand and cupped her face. "We've just met, but I'm a good judge of character, and I can already tell you're a wonderful woman. I want to know everything about you. Nothing you could say would change what I think of you, Lily." A feathery kiss on the forehead sealed the deal.

She took in a deep breath, then the words tumbled out. "What if I told you I killed my sister?"

CHAPTER 8

Natalie Lyons exited her Mercedes SUV and kicked the mounds of caked snow from under the wheel wells, then stamped clean her UGGs before entering the house through the garage.

It wasn't as fruitful a day as she would have liked, but she did discover that the private dick, Aiden O'Rourke, stopped in to see the sheriff, and that he stayed precisely forty-six minutes.

"Nat? That you?" came her mother's voice. Then the clicking of stilettos on polished marble.

"Yeah, Mom. It's me," she answered in her usual flat tone.

Gabrielle Lyons poked a coiffed blonde head around the corner as Natalie hung her jacket and removed her boots.

Mother and daughter were a study in contrasts. Natalie, nineteen, was tall and reedy with long arms and legs that gave her an insect-like appearance. Dull brown hair hung unkempt around a long, bony face. Blue eyes, bright as chips of lapis lazuli, were her only redeeming feature.

Gabrielle was shorter and had some meat on her forty-six-year-old bones, but she was beautiful; there was no denying that. She'd bought herself a nose job, hair extensions, veneers for her teeth, new boobs, and a facelift. A tummy tuck and lipo were next on her list.

"What did you find out?" Gabrielle's voice was thick with anticipation.

Natalie shrugged. "The private dick went to see the sheriff. I sat for almost an hour outside the station freezing my buns off."

Natalie feigned disinterest for her mother's benefit, but in truth she'd been compelled to watch and follow Aiden O'Rourke. She needed to know where he was and what he was doing. "Keep your friends close and your enemies closer" was one of her dad's favorite sayings, and Natalie knew it to be good advice. It also comforted her, made her feel she had control over something in her life.

After Aiden left the sheriff's office, Natalie had parked outside Lily's house. Watching Lily was her other obsession. Then surprise, surprise, Miss Valier hopped into her Corolla and hightailed it up that long and winding road to Aiden's cozy cabin in the woods.

Why was he spending time with that whore? Although she didn't know Lily well, she reasoned she wouldn't be much different than her slut of a sister. Since Aiden wasn't exactly hard on the eyes, Natalie understood Lily's attraction to the man, and she'd heard how he'd saved her from a burglary the other night. No doubt he was an instant hero in Lily's eyes.

"So, nothing to report? You don't know what that private eye talked to the sheriff about?"

God, her mother could be a nosey pain in the ass. She sighed. "All I know is that he was there." She left out the details as she strutted past. Her mother didn't care as much as she let on about her husband's well-being, so the less Gabrielle knew, the better. Still, Natalie had to walk a fine line to keep her mother happy, giving her just enough info so the bucks would continue to flow and Deputy Deluca would remain firmly planted in her pocket. With a trust fund locked down tight until she was twenty-five, getting her hands on a lot of dough was impossible.

"You'd better call that deputy. Find out if he knows anything. Or do you want me to?" Gabrielle asked.

Natalie held up a hand. "No. I'll do it." She headed for the kitchen with Gabrielle trailing and took a seat at the counter. "Where's Daddy?"

"At the office, but he'll be home for dinner." Gabrielle sidled up beside her daughter and plucked a red velvet cupcake from a silver-tiered tower. She placed it in front of Natalie and smiled. "Stop worrying. Everything will be fine."

Natalie turned to her mother, pushing the cupcake away. "Daddy was questioned once. He could be questioned again, especially with that PI in town. Right now, the sheriff thinks he was away on business when Sara Valier was killed, and we both know that's not true. If they find out, that'll make him look guilty."

Her dad, though far from perfect, gave her more than her mother ever did. He'd actually said the words "I love you" and even called her pet names from time to time. As far as Natalie was concerned, her mother was made of solid ice. It had always been that way, as far back as she could remember. Life wouldn't be worth living without her dad. He was the only one who could cool the fires of fury that often burned in her, and give her a hand up when depression swept her into its depths. Nothing, and no one else, could help, not even the antidepressants the doctors kept trying to force down her throat.

Gabrielle's lips pressed into a grim line. "I'm sick of this." She shook her head solemnly. "If they do, then they do. We're doing all we can to protect your dad, but he is a grown man, and maybe he should face the consequences of his actions."

Natalie felt her face darken like a thundercloud, and her hands fisted in anger. Infidelity was one thing and, unfortunately, her mother made sure she knew her dad was guilty of that, but murder was something else entirely. "Daddy didn't do it." Her words were emphatic.

Gabrielle patted her daughter's back and sighed. "I'm sorry. All I'm saying is, it's not fair that he put us in this position. Damn him anyway." She slapped a palm on the granite counter top, her rings clinking against the stone surface.

Tears brimmed in Natalie's eyes. "I don't know what I'd do if anything ever happened to Daddy."

A frown would have creased Gabrielle's forehead if she hadn't had a Botox injection that week. "I know you love him, but he can be a bastard, Natalie. You're old enough to know that. He's far from perfect." She bit into a vanilla cupcake, icing dotting the end of her nose.

"He's perfect to me," Natalie whispered.

Gabrielle sighed heavily and got up. "Got to check on Angela. She should be in here starting dinner." She clicked her way out of the kitchen in search of the hired help.

When her mother was out of sight, Natalie made her way to the powder room and locked the door. She opened a drawer and fished through her mother's various pill bottles, finally settling on one. Popping open the lid, she tapped out two small pills onto her palm and dry swallowed them. Who needed antidepressants when painkillers did a better job?

She sat on the lid of the toilet seat and fished her cell out of her pocket. Soon her troubles would float away, at least for a few hours. A respite from the world and from reality was sorely needed. "Please, God, don't let Daddy get into any more trouble," she whispered before hitting the first number on her speed dial.

"Yeah?" Antonio Deluca answered on the first ring.

"Can you talk?" Natalie asked.

"Just a sec."

She heard footfalls as he went in search of privacy.

"OK, I'm back, but I don't have much time." Deluca spoke in a hushed tone and there was a slight echo to his voice, making Natalie think he was in the men's room.

Yuck, she thought, and got straight to the point. "I know Aiden O'Rourke was at the station today. Why didn't you phone me?"

"I was going to. Give me a chance, will ya?"

She ignored his annoyance. "Did you hear anything?"

"Only the usual."

"And that is…?" Now annoyance was in her voice. Did she have to pull every word out of him? Antonio was quiet by nature, but the hundred-dollar bills she kept doling out to him were meant to loosen his lips.

"You know I've done all I can to put Wilkins on Lily Valier's trail. Don't worry, your dear old dad won't go down for this. I've got him thinking Lily did it."

Relief flooded her. However short-lived it might be, she was grateful for it.

"Anything else?"

"O'Rourke's going to question Phil Kemp. You know him? The guy Sara Valier was seeing before your dad? Personally, I think it's a waste of time. He's innocent. Oh, and O'Rourke's got plans with Lily for tonight. Sounds like he's got her wrapped around his little finger."

"I know who Phil Kemp is," Natalie said, exasperation tingeing her voice. "I guess that's a logical place to start." But now the knot of worry tightened like a noose around her neck, choking her with panic. Her dad was sure to be on O'Rourke's list, because that was the *next* logical step. Her only hope was her dad would be smart enough to outwit the PI.

As for Lily being wrapped around Aiden's finger, that'd be an easy finger to get wrapped around, but what good would it do him? Phil Kemp may be innocent, but Natalie knew Lily was too.

CHAPTER 9

Aiden was bewildered. Was she confessing? He had to say something, but what? An awkward silence stretched out before them.

Lily must have noticed the shock on his face, because she spoke before he could gather his wits enough to form a question. "You might as well know. You'll find out eventually anyway." She watched him, seemingly for a reaction.

"You didn't kill your sister," he said, though it was more of a question than a statement.

Lily looked away, but Aiden put a hand under her chin and turned her back to him. "Why did you say that?"

She looked contrite and shifted uncomfortably. "Everyone in this town thinks I killed Sara. I...I wanted to see if you thought I was capable of such a horrendous thing."

He'd have to pretend to be the devoted potential boyfriend if he was going to get more out of her. "I could never imagine you capable of killing anyone, let alone your own sister." Aiden injected concern into his voice and looked at her tenderly.

Lily gave a wavering smile. "That means a lot."

"This is pretty heavy stuff we're talking about, but if I'm going to get to know you, I want to know *all* about you. It'll go both ways. I'm an open book too. You can ask me anything and tell me anything." He laid a comforting hand on her shoulder. "Would it be OK if I asked some more questions?" For a second he wanted to cringe. Was he pushing too hard?

Lily shrugged. "It can't hurt now. By the end of this evening you'll either kick me out of your house or be one of my only friends." She laughed, though he noted it was without humor.

Aiden could think of no way to soften the next question, but did manage a sympathetic expression to accompany it. One he almost felt. "How was she killed?"

"Shot."

He was surprised by the directness of the answer but pleased. "God! I'm so sorry." Another tender look.

Lily sighed and wrapped both hands around her plastic cup. "I might as well save you from having to ask a million questions," she said, staring into the wine. "Sara was five months pregnant when she was murdered. Shot in the throat and bled to death. Her body was found on the kitchen floor at her house. Unfortunately, I was the last one to see her alive…and…" She hesitated as if the next few words were the hardest of all. "And, the murder weapon was more than likely my gun." She raised her gaze to meet his. "Now can you see why I'm a suspect?"

"More than likely your gun? What does that mean?"

Lily waved a dismissive hand. "Doesn't matter."

Like hell it didn't matter, he wanted to say. That gun was the missing puzzle piece to the crime. "Doesn't the sheriff have the murder weapon?" He needed to keep her talking. How he wished he could come right out and ask if she had the gun, or knew where it was, but of course he couldn't. Right now, he had to go along with her and act as if he believed every word.

"No."

Damn one-word answers! Aiden's hope was fading. "Why would the sheriff think you'd want to kill your own sister?"

A bark of laughter erupted from her. "There's a very good reason." She eyed him hard. "For the money. Dad left his millions to Sara. I got nothing."

"Wow," he said, running a hand through his hair. He contemplated asking how much money was involved and why her dad shut her out of the inheritance. Wouldn't that be the logical follow-up? No, he decided, it would be too personal. He changed tack. "I guess I can understand why you were under suspicion, but it's all cleared up now, right? Does the sheriff have any leads?"

Wilkins had already given him the information she'd just revealed, but somehow it was different hearing it from her. Venom colored her voice. Could Lily have actually hated her sister because of what their father did, or maybe it was a heat-of-the-moment thing? Damn it, but she *was* the most likely suspect. He looked at her green eyes blazing, lips pressed into a line of agitation, and let out the breath he hadn't realized he was holding. Why was he disappointed?

"I was taken into custody and questioned. Hired a lawyer and, in the end, they only had circumstantial evidence. Not enough to charge me. But I know they still have their eyes on me. I'm innocent and there's no goddamn way I'm going to feel uncomfortable in my own town." She drained her glass again, and it made him think of the night he'd sicced Chrome on her and how she'd handily slammed back that Scotch. Then she added, "Besides, leaving town now would only make me look guilty."

Lily picked up the bottle but put it back down when she saw it was empty.

Aiden stood. "I'll open another."

She waved a hand to indicate she'd had enough. "No, it's OK."

Plucking up their cups and the empty bottle, Aiden placed them on the tray. "Come keep me company in the kitchen while I get dinner ready."

* * *

Lily sat on a stool at the counter, another plastic cup of wine in front of her. It had been some time since she'd had so much to drink, but it felt good. She needed this, needed someone she could loosen up with. "Need help with anything?" she asked from her perch.

Aiden stirred the tomato sauce that was bubbling softly in a pot, then set another filled with water on the burner next to it. "No, I've got everything covered. The sauce is done and all I have to do is cook the pasta." He looked apologetic. "It's nothing fancy."

"Just having someone else doing the cooking is more than enough for me." She smiled.

"If you don't mind me asking, I'm curious about the father of Sara's baby. You never mentioned him, but from what I've learned from cop shows, isn't the boyfriend or husband always the first suspect?"

She wasn't surprised when Aiden turned the conversation back to her sister's murder. It was a bit exasperating, but she'd answer. "Sara was having an affair with a married man named Zander Lyons. Zander and Sara broke up a little while after she got pregnant. He wasn't going to leave his wife and wanted Sara to have an abortion. She refused. Sheriff Wilkins knows all this, but Zander's alibi is apparently ironclad." The words rolled off her tongue in a matter-of-fact tone. Show no emotion, she told herself. It's easier that way.

"Was Sara scared of him?"

Lily shrugged. "I don't know, but Zander's a real ass. He's the show-offy type with a big ego, thinks he's in charge of everything and everyone. Like a spoiled rich kid, used to getting his way. I do remember Sara telling me something creepy he'd said—that one way or another, she was going to lose the baby. That's a threat if ever I heard one. But Sara never actually *said* she was afraid of him." Lily huffed. "My sister didn't always tell me everything. Don't get me wrong; we were close. She was like a mother to me. Always taking care of everything, but sometimes she kept things to herself so I wouldn't worry. That's the feeling I got when it came to Zander Lyons."

"Is there anyone else you can think of who would want your sister dead? Think hard. Anyone at all?"

She wrinkled her nose and shook her head. "God, you sound like a cop. Too many crime shows maybe?"

"I'm sorry. I just want to help. Am I getting too personal? Tell me if I am, OK?" He added the pasta to the boiling water. "Listen, dinner will be ready soon. Do you want to talk about something else?"

She thought about Philip Kemp. Should she mention him? He'd seen her with the gun the day Sara was murdered. Maybe it would be better not to bring up his name.

"That's a good idea. Enough about me." She raised a brow and fixed him with a look of hard suspicion. "Tell me what you really do for a living, and don't say stockbroker."

CHAPTER 10

Aiden swallowed his panic and laughed. "Of course I'm a stockbroker. Or rather, *was* a stockbroker. Retired now, remember?"

Lily leaned closer and cocked her head. "Really?"

He nodded, perhaps a little too vigorously. The intensity of her stare was unnerving. It made him want to keep talking to try to convince her. Aiden squared his shoulders and returned her gaze. He took a deep breath and said, "OK, OK, I'm a detective." Then he gave her his best dimple-popping smile when he saw the shock on her face. "Gotcha!"

She returned his smile. "Good one."

Relief filled him. She was a lot smarter than he'd thought. How could he keep questioning her without raising suspicion? Aiden turned away and stirred the pasta, pulling out a strand for a taste test. "Al dente," he declared while chewing. "Hope that's how you like it."

He'd set the table with the only dishes in the cabin. They were white with a blue border and so thin they were almost transparent. He thought they might be those dishes that were so popular in the seventies. The ones that could be dropped and wouldn't shatter. The place setting was nothing fancy, but while he was out he'd picked up a couple of candle holders and tapers from the dollar store to add to the ambience.

Aiden sparked a match and lit the candles, secretly praying they weren't a fire hazard, then turned down the dimmer switch in the kitchen. The aroma of wine, basil, garlic, and the scent of burning logs mingled, stirring him, making him feel as if he was on a real date.

The pale of Lily's eyes reflected the glow of the candles. Her hair shone, casting a halo around her head and shoulders, and the curve of her lips made him want to pull her to him and kiss her deeply. It made him want other things too. Perhaps later.

"What are you thinking?" she asked, catching the smile he'd been trying to hide.

How beautiful she was and how he wanted her more than he'd wanted any woman in a very long time. "That I'm pretty damn hungry."

She smiled, biting her lower lip as she took a seat at the table. He noticed the cling of her blouse around full breasts and caught a peek at the black lace beneath it. It'd be easy to kiss her now, maybe slide a hand under that silk.

"Hey, did you make the meatballs from scratch?" Lily asked, and he was glad for the diversion.

"Absolutely," he lied as he set the bowl of pasta in the center of the table along with a fresh-cut French loaf.

Over dinner, Aiden kept to chitchat, nattering on about his childhood, most of which was true. It was easier to infuse real life into the conversation, that way he wouldn't have to remember so many lies. He told her about his younger sister, Nora, and how he missed her since she and her family moved to California because of her husband's job. Then about his father's heart attack three years ago and his mother's car accident. He tried his best to just be a regular guy. Of course he'd thrown in *some* lies. He'd had time to make up a backstory about his career and added a fictional close call with marriage just for the fun of it. He told Lily, with feigned heartfelt conviction, how much he wanted to settle down and have kids, and that a small town like Higgstown was the perfect place to raise a family.

"How did you know she wasn't the right one for you? If you wanted to get married so badly, wasn't it difficult to call it off?" Lily asked, her eyes wide with interest.

He had her now. "I want to get married more than anything in the world. I want a wife. I want kids, but I refuse to settle. I need a woman who'll challenge me every day. I like adventure in a relationship and Melissa just didn't do that for me." Aiden held her gaze and reached for her hand. He was laying it on thick, telling her what every woman wanted to hear from a man. "You've been kicking my ass all night, Miss Valier. You just might be the kind of woman I'm looking for."

He noticed she hadn't touched the wine he'd poured for her before dinner. It was looking as if she was trying to keep her wits about her.

She smiled at his words and looked for a moment as if she was going to speak, but then something changed in her expression. It was as if a switch had been thrown and the light in her eyes went out. Lily patted her lips with a napkin and pushed her chair back to stand. "Maybe I should go? It's getting late and with the snow and all…" She turned to look out the window.

Shit! He still needed answers, but where could he go from here? He'd already tried the direct approach, but that only raised her suspicions. Then he turned on the charm, and now she was running for the hills. He took a deep breath, collected himself, walked to the kitchen window, and flicked on the outside light. Flakes were still falling, fat and thick. The snow he'd cleared earlier had been replenished and with a bit more to boot.

"I really hate to say this, but it doesn't look like you'll be going anywhere tonight." He turned back to face her, suddenly relieved. Maybe he'd have another chance to gain her trust.

Lily stood beside him and peered out the window. Sure enough there had to be a foot of newly fallen snow. Her car was practically buried. There'd be no way to get back down that driveway. What the hell was she doing here anyway?

The evening had been a strange one. She couldn't put her finger on it, but something wasn't sitting right with her. Aiden was, of course, amazing, cute, and desirable. Every time she looked at those lips she wanted to kiss them, but could she trust him? Wilkins and Deluca were handling the murder investigation, so she was pretty sure he wasn't a cop. But a stockbroker? The more she got to know him, the more unlikely it seemed.

She gave her head a shake and put her suspicions on the back burner, but what was she going to do about getting home?

"Why don't you stay? You can have my bed, and I'll sleep on the couch," Aiden suggested.

His words pulled her from her thoughts. "No, I couldn't. Besides, I have Rex to think about." Although he'd more than likely already had an accident or two on the dining room rug. Jesus Christ! What choice did she have?

"Lily, please. Have a look out there. When the morning comes, I'll clear the snow down to the road so you can get home. And I promise I won't try anything, really." He pouted and that made her smile.

"OK," she relented, and an unexpected tingle of excitement ran up her spine.

He stepped closer and kissed her. "That's all you're going to get out of me, young lady. No more. I'm not that kind of man."

They sat in front of the fire and chatted until her lids grew heavy. She'd let him do most of the talking, and she was relieved he hadn't asked any more personal questions.

She wanted to trust Aiden and had every intention of giving him the benefit of the doubt, but it had to be at a pace she was comfortable with.

A sudden thought struck that maybe the storm was a sign they should be together. Yes, she decided, that was how she was going to take it. They had no choice but to spend a lot of time together, getting to know one another. He seemed so sincere. What she'd felt earlier were just her silly demons popping up.

The fire was dwindling now, but she was glad for it. The heat had made her sleepy. Leaning her head on Aiden's shoulder, Lily stifled a yawn, and he wrapped an arm around her. It felt so right, so natural. Then his lips where on hers, and she kissed him back, all thoughts of sleep falling away. He let his hand slip from around her shoulders, fingers now inching closer to her breasts. Instinctively, she moved nearer. He unbuttoned her blouse, and she felt the silk of it as it fell from her shoulders. A shudder of pleasure ran through her.

God, she wanted more. *Needed* more.

"Wanna go upstairs?" he asked between kisses.

"Yes, yes," she whispered.

CHAPTER 11

After they'd made love, Lily lounged in Aiden's arms. The even rhythm of his breath, his scent, the warmth of his body, the solidness of him made her feel as if she were finally home and without a care in the world. Once he'd nodded off, she lifted her head to peek at him. He was like a masterpiece sculpted out of marble. Chiseled jawline and a square, angular face with a hint of stubble. She could gaze at him all night, but the lull of contentment was dragging her to sleep's door.

The bed was simple, made of pine like the rest of the cabin. It was large, king size, but she didn't want her own space. She wanted to meld into him. There was no fluffy duvet, no overstuffed pillows, only sheets and a thin blanket. Despite her contentment, the chill in the air forced Lily out of bed in search of something to don. The floorboards creaked as she made her way to the armoire on tippy toes. She could barely make out its shape in the dim light of the moon shining through the sheers.

Finding the armoire at last, she carefully pulled the door open, relieved it made no sound. Lily felt around in the darkness for something warm, hoping for a sweatshirt. Her hand landed on a few T-shirts and a pair of jeans thrown haphazardly onto a shelf. A neat man Aiden was not. She smiled as she refolded the clothes and stacked them in a tidy pile.

Shivering, she peered around in search of a closet. Perhaps something warmer would be hanging in there. Then she remembered the flannel shirt Aiden had been wearing earlier, the one with the snaps she wanted to rip open. That brought a smile as she thought of how she'd ended up doing just that. A wave of desire rippled through her as she recalled the feel of his chest, smooth and firm under her hands and then her lips.

The shirt lay in a heap on the floor by his side of the bed, and she walked over to scoop it up. She brought it to her face for a moment. It was soft and smelled like burned wood and cologne. As she donned it, Lily noticed Aiden's jeans and picked them up too. With the jeans folded over an arm, she made her way back to the armoire to put them away. Something in the pocket moved! Lily almost dropped them until she realized it was the familiar vibration of a cell phone and fished it from his pocket.

A name glowed brightly on the screen and for a second she worried the light would wake Aiden, but when she saw the name of the caller, Lily went limp, dropping the phone along with the jeans. Bile rose hot in her throat as her legs threatened to give way under her. No! a voice screamed in her head.

The light on the night table clicked on. "What's wrong?" Aiden jumped to his feet, a sheet clutched around his waist.

Lily pointed to the phone lying at his feet. "You bastard! You son of a bitch." She pulled off the thin blanket from the bed and wrapped it around herself. Anger had her firmly in its grasp as she bent to pick up the phone and hold it out to him. "You gonna answer it?"

Aiden looked at it and shook his head just as it stilled. "I can explain…" He held his hand out to her, but she ignored it, stepping backward, feeling for her own clothes without taking her eyes from him.

"There's nothing to explain." Her hand closed on her blouse and pants, and she turned away to quickly dress. "All those damn questions. I should have known," she chided herself. "Jesus, how stupid can I be?" Lily turned back to face him. "Did you have to sleep with me? Did you have to use me too?"

Aiden sat heavily on the bed, the mattress creaking in protest. "You…I… This was real," he said, eyes downcast.

"None of this is real, Aiden. This is all bullshit. Is Aiden even your name? Who are you, *really*?"

"A detective. And yes, Aiden's my name." His tone seemed earnest, but she didn't care. There was no trusting him now.

"So, Wilkins hired you?" She launched the phone at him, hitting his shoulder. It bounced off him and onto the bed. "Guess you didn't get what you wanted, did you? You thought you could seduce me and get me to confess to killing Sara." She made her way to the staircase and turned back toward him. "Well, you seduced me, so congratulations on getting half the job done."

"Wait!" He sprang up behind her, the sheet trailing him. He clamped a hand around her arm. "Where are you going?"

With a look of indignation, Lily wrenched free. "Home. You don't think I'm going to stay the night?"

"Let me get dressed and we can talk." He backed away slowly, keeping an eye on her. "Please. I'll explain everything."

She gave a harsh bark of laughter and started down the stairs.

* * *

Lily was at the front door donning her coat when Aiden came up behind her after dressing. He had no choice but to lay all his cards on the table. "I'm sorry you had to find out this way, but for what it's worth, I don't think you killed your sister, and I'd like to help find who did." He watched for a reaction, hoping she'd see reason.

Lily stopped fussing with the zipper of her coat, but when she looked at him, he saw only contempt.

"Can we talk? I'll tell you everything you want to know." He gestured to the living room where just moments ago they'd been happy.

She kept her coat on but took off her boots, walked to the living room without a word, and settled into a corner of one of the couches, sending a message she wanted him nowhere near her. Aiden sat on the other couch and pulled the throw over his shoulders. The fire had guttered out, leaving a crisp chill in the air. How was he going to talk his way out of this? Although he'd told Lily he thought she was innocent, that wasn't entirely true. He *hoped* she was innocent despite the evidence pointing decidedly in her direction.

He eyed the woman he'd just made love to. She was beautiful even when furious, even when hatred burned in her eyes, even if she was a murderer.

"Should I make coffee? To warm us up?"

"No, goddamn it. You said you were going to explain, so start talking." She pulled up her legs and hugged her knees to herself.

"OK." He held up a hand. "You've figured out Wilkins hired me. That's true, but I'm here to find your sister's murderer, so try to look at this as a positive. If you didn't do it—and I don't think you did—we can work together. If we team up…"

"Bullshit. You would have been honest with me from the start if that's what you really wanted to do. You think I'm guilty just like everyone else in this town."

"That was before I knew you." He edged forward and tilted his head to catch her gaze. "We've only known each other a short while, but I'm a good judge of character, and I don't think you're capable of murder. But there are two men who were in your sister's life at the time of her death, and we've got to find out if either one of them could be. What can you tell me about Philip Kemp and Zander Lyons? Things you haven't told me yet."

She looked surprised. "You know about Philip?"

"All I know is that he was seeing your sister before her affair with Zander."

Lily exhaled audibly. "I don't want to talk about him."

"Please, Lily, I want to help." He reached out and traced a finger over her hand, but she jerked away. Slow down, he told himself. She's a hard nut to crack, remember?

CHAPTER 12

Natalie Lyons sat at the bottom of Ryan's Road, positioned in the perfect spot to be able to see Aiden's cabin. How the hell that woman got to the top of the driveway in this weather was beyond her. Lily must have been more than a little desperate to see that hunky PI.

After tucking her phone away in her jacket pocket, she checked her gas gauge. The needle dipped lower than she was comfortable with, but it was either keep the car running or freeze her ass off, so she opted for warming her ass. She could see that a light was on in the lower level of the cabin. A quick glance at her dash revealed 3:34 shining in a peaceful blue glow. "Guess it's an all-nighter," she said in disgust, then glimpsed herself in the rear-view mirror— mousy brown hair hung limp and lifeless across her face, making her hate herself all the more. Natalie turned, slipped the SUV into gear, and drove away.

Tomorrow she'd plant another seed.

* * *

"Where the hell were you?" Zander asked when she entered the house. Her dad was sitting on the steps at the bottom of the large, winding staircase waiting for her to come home, a ragged copy of Stephen King's *The Stand* in hand.

"Out."

"Out! I almost called the sheriff. And do you know what it would take for me to call that bastard?" She knew but ignored the question.

"Mommy sleeping?"

Zander grunted. "Of course. Do you think she'd be worried enough about you to stay up till all hours of the morning? Your mom's not concerned about your welfare like I am." He sighed and shook his shaggy head. "Remember what happened almost a year ago? When you ran your car off the road?" He didn't give her a chance to respond. "You broke your collarbone and ended up with a concussion."

Natalie did remember and despite her best efforts to look disinterested, she let her head hang. She'd done it on purpose, wanting the attention, and was well aware her dad knew this. He was acquainted with the demons that lived inside her. She also knew her mother couldn't have stayed up for her even if she tried. Her nasty habit of "a sleeping pill a day keeps the nightmares away" took care of that.

"Goddamn it, Natalie." Zander slammed the dog-eared novel down beside him, a lock of brown hair falling across his eyes, and stood. "I'm gonna ask one more time. Where...were...you?"

She tossed her keys into the bowl on the foyer table and tucked an errant strand of hair behind an ear. "Just got things on my mind is all. I needed some alone time." She strode past him without so much as glancing his way.

Never the perfect child, she knew she was a worry with her moodiness, her instability, and the things she did to shock people, like the piercings and tattoos. Doctor after doctor was unable to help. In her most private thoughts, she wondered if something was wrong with her and if her dad thought the same thing. Something that couldn't be fixed.

Zander let out a frustrated sigh. "Nat, you're the only one who believes I'm innocent of that awful crime." He was trying to win her over, pull her out of her *mood*. Swinging the conversation back to him—her poor old dad. She could almost read his mind. Gabby, his ice queen of a wife, thought he was capable of murder and she, his ever-loving daughter, was all he had left.

Natalie noticed the ten-carat canary-diamond ring with matching earrings he'd bought her mother after the Sara Valier murder. She'd also heard their fight. Her dad begging her mother not to leave. Probably cheaper than a divorce she figured. Still, she was glad when her mother stayed despite the continued chill in the air.

Zander followed her into the great room. He wasn't really angry with her anymore. She could feel it. Natalie lay down on the couch and flicked on the TV.

"Are you looking for Sara's killer?" he asked, his tone softer.

She turned the volume to mute and rolled over to face him. "No."

She knew that lie as well as he did. Zander moved her legs over to sit beside her. "Let the cops do their job."

Natalie sat up. "If I don't do what I can to help, they might come after you again."

Tears sprang to her eyes and he pulled her into an embrace.

"Honey, I've been cleared." He held her at arm's length and studied her. "You know I didn't do it, right?"

She was quick to nod. "I know. But what if they can't find out who did it? They're going to want to pin it on someone, and you're the most…logical."

Zander smiled. "Now how are they going to do that without any evidence?"

She hesitated, then answered with a weak smile of her own, "I guess you're right."

"I don't want you out at all hours of the night. You've got to let go of this. As long as I'm in the clear there's nothing to worry about, OK?"

The words "there is something to worry about" lingered on her lips, but she swallowed them. How could she tell him all she knew?

CHAPTER 13

Dinally & Sons Auto and Tires was dingy and small, surrounded by a mountain of old tires and a cemetery of car parts. Some Aiden recognized and some were so old and rusted out, they just looked like garbage. The sign on the building was huge and painted in fading black. It read: Dinally & Sons since 1945. Because Philip Kemp was neither a Dinally nor old enough to have started the business himself, Aiden suspected he'd bought it from the original owner.

It looked as if it may have been successful in its day. The old brick building was painted in a now peeling and fading yellow, and Aiden tried to picture it as it would have looked way back when, in all its sunny glory.

The parking lot wasn't plowed, but part of it was shoveled free of snow. Aiden pulled into a spot between snowbanks and got out of his truck. At first glance, it looked deserted, but a faint clanging of metal on metal led him to the side of the building where a bay door was up and a lone man worked on the underside of an ancient truck on a hoist.

"Hey there," Aiden called.

The man stopped and turned. "Mornin'. How can I help you?" A little twang colored his voice. A southerner, Aiden figured and smiled. He strode closer. "I'm looking for Philip Kemp. You wouldn't happen to be him, would you?"

The man wiped his right hand on grease-stained coveralls. "Yeah, I'm Phil." He held out a not entirely clean hand in greeting. Tall and athletic looking, he wore a white cotton T-shirt under his coveralls. Ropey muscles glistened with sweat despite the bite in the air.

After shaking Philip's hand, Aiden nonchalantly wiped the oily residue transferred in the handshake onto his own jeans, grateful he wasn't wearing his good pair. "My name's Aiden O'Rourke. Can I steal a few minutes of your time?"

Philip's eyes narrowed and Aiden took note he hadn't yet put down the heavy-looking wrench he'd been using when he got there. Instead, his hand fisted around it, tightening the muscles in his sinewy forearms.

"What's this about?" Philip turned back to the truck and began working again.

Despite his holstered gun, Aiden couldn't help but be relieved when it seemed Philip had no intention of using the wrench on him. He understood what Sara saw in the man, in a raw, sexual sort of way. Philip was tall and well built with sandy blond hair and chiseled features. His guess was she had only been with him out of good old-fashioned animal attraction. Didn't look like he had a dime to his name and judging by the number of cars in the garage, that being the old man of a truck on the hoist, he didn't have much by way of prospects either.

"I'm a detective, Mr. Kemp. I'm here to ask a few questions about the murder of Sara Valier." Aiden pulled a badge from his back pocket and flashed it long enough for Philip to have a look.

An echoing clang rang through the open space, making Aiden leap back a step. Philip had dropped the wrench, and its unfortunate landing on a metal grate added considerably to the decibel level.

"Sorry." His blue eyes clouded with tears, and he wiped them away on the short sleeve of his shirt. "I already spoke to the sheriff." His gaze was focused on the far wall, but Aiden suspected he wasn't really *seeing* anything, only feeling and remembering. But what? That was the question.

"The case is still open. I've been called in to help out. It would really mean a lot if you'd give me a few minutes of your time."

Philip nodded toward a door, and Aiden began to follow when he walked away. They made their way from the bay into the building through a battered steel door that housed a broken pane of glass. One that looked as if it would shatter with a not-so-hard slam. Once inside, Philip led Aiden to a tiny walk-through kitchen that was more of a hallway than a room. Old newspapers were stacked high, empty takeout food containers and greasy car parts littered the area, and the sour scent of rotten food and old motor oil hung thickly in the air.

"Coffee?" Philip poured himself a cup that looked as thick as molasses to Aiden.

He waved a hand. "Ah, no thanks there, buddy."

They sat at a small table that had been shoved up against a wall. Aiden had to climb over a mountain of crap to get to a grease-stained chair. Again, he was glad to be wearing his old jeans, the ones with the rip in the knee and now a smear of grease on the right leg.

"So, whatta ya wanna know?" Philip asked as he slurped his coffee.

"How long did you know Ms. Valier?"

"Six months." Philip turned away to look out a dingy window. The gray slats of a blind had been haphazardly yanked up and hung almost vertically, obscuring Aiden's view of what he figured was a junkyard. "I wanted to marry her. I loved Sara."

Aiden wasn't surprised to see tears standing in Philip's eyes again.

"OK, good to know." He was being flippant, yes, but the guy was a gusher. "How did you two meet?"

"Through a friend."

Aiden took out a notebook and a pen from his jacket. "Mind if I write this down?"

"What for? I told ya I didn't kill her." Philip's brows smashed together in worry. "You believe me, don't ya?"

"Of course. I just want to get things right...the things you tell me, so I can find the killer."

"Then you oughta go talk to that sister of hers. She's the murderer. I can tell you that right now."

Aiden looked up from his pad and cleared his throat. "And you know this how?"

"I was there when she, Lily's her name, when Lily pulled a gun on Sara."

Although Aiden already knew this, hearing it from Philip's lips made it more real, more concrete, and more damning for Lily. "Tell me exactly where you were when you saw Lily pull the gun."

A crimson flush began to work its way up Philip's neck, giving him the look of a man who wanted to be anywhere but where he was at the moment. "Um, well, this might sound kinda weird and like I said, I already told the sheriff all this, but anyways, I was sitting in my car, across the street from Lily's house."

"Why?"

Philip tugged at his shirt as if it was suddenly too tight. "I ain't no stalker. Only wanted to see Sara, so I followed her and that's where she went—to her sister's house. I sat in my car waiting on her and then they came outside and talked for a while in the front yard. All of a sudden, Lily ran back in the house and I saw Sara get in her car, like she was gonna drive away. When Lily came back out, she had a gun in her hand. She pulled open Sara's car door and I heard Sara yell 'no'."

"Did either of the women see you?"

Philip shook his head.

"So what happened next? Did you actually *see* Lily pointing the gun at her sister?"

Pursed lips and a knitted brow made it look as if thinking was painful. "Yup, I think so."

"You think? You mean to tell me you can't say with one hundred percent certainty you saw Lily pointing a gun at Sara?"

Philip's face became a thundercloud. "I know what I saw and yes, I did see her lift that gun up and point it right at Sara. And that's what I told Sheriff Wilkins later on, you know, after Sara was killed. I sent him an e-mail."

Aiden nodded. "I've seen the e-mail, but there's something puzzling me." He cocked a brow and stared hard into Philip's blue eyes.

"What's that?" Philip asked tentatively.

"Why didn't you do anything?"

The flush crept farther up Philip's neck until it colored his cheeks. "'Cause…'cause I was caught off guard, and besides it all happened so quick."

Aiden knew without asking why Philip hadn't gotten out of his car to help Sara, and he let him know. "You didn't help because you were too chickenshit to get involved. You saw the gun, and you got the hell outta there."

Tears were back and Philip pinched them away with blackened fingers, leaving an absurd-looking smear across the bridge of his nose. He stared silently down at his feet.

Aiden spoke louder this time. "Answer me, Philip. You left, didn't you?"

Philip snapped his head up, gave Aiden a quick glance, then looked away. "Yeah, I left. You satisfied now? I didn't have the guts to save the woman I loved. That what you wanna hear?"

A smile found its way onto Aiden's lips. Yes, that was what he wanted to hear, exactly what he wanted to hear. There was a huge crack in Philip's story and that meant a ray of hope for Lily, tiny as it might be. Philip may have seen a gun, but he hadn't stuck around to see much of anything else. Anything could have happened after he left. Lily and Sara could have made up, that is if they'd even been fighting. From what Philip had just described, it didn't sound like much of a fight to Aiden.

"A few more questions and I'll let you get back to work. Aside from hearing Sara say 'no', did you hear anything else? Did Lily say anything?"

Philip's eyes held a faraway look as if his mind had drifted back to that day. "Um, I know she was speaking. I could see Lily's lips moving and she was real animated. She was saying something, but I couldn't quite make it out. Windows were up and I had the AC on. It was a scorcher of a day."

"But you did hear Sara say 'no'? You're sure of that?"

"Oh yeah. She yelled it. Even with the windows up, I heard her loud and clear."

"How long would you estimate you were there watching all this going on?"

Philip picked absently at a greasy fingernail, wiping what he fished out onto the knee of his coveralls. "Ten minutes."

Aiden didn't need to take up any more of the man's time. "Thanks, Mr. Kemp. I appreciate you answering my questions."

Philip was just a pretty boy with the IQ of a sack of potatoes. He wasn't the killer. Still, there was the matter of what happened to the gun. Where was it? It was what Wilkins and Deluca needed in order to match the slugs from Sara's neck to the murder weapon. Without it, they had nothing.

Aiden thought briefly about asking Philip Kemp to put a set of snows on his truck but thought better of it. It didn't feel right. After all, he'd just made the man cry. Several times. Best he get out of there and let him have some privacy.

Like it or not, he was going to have to question Lily about her fight with Sara, and then it would be time to pay Zander Lyons a visit.

CHAPTER 14

Lily had never in her life been happier to be back in her own element, the diner. Annie greeted her with a big smile and a "tell me everything" look, but with a shake of her head and pursed lips, Lily's expression said it all. Annie's smile went out; returning Lily's sad expression, Annie passed with hands full of breakfast orders. "I'm here if you need to talk."

Although grateful for the offer, Lily didn't think she'd be able to or want to give Annie the details just yet. She made her way to her office and plopped into her desk chair.

Before coming to work, she'd stopped by to let Rex out and clean up the accidents he'd had during the night. She couldn't really blame him. After all, he'd been alone for hours. He'd met her at the door with that guilty look only dogs could manage. It made her smile and broke her heart all at the same time, poor thing. She'd been neglecting him lately.

Work was her solace now. It was a distraction from the horrible night she'd been forced to spend at Aiden's. The fury she'd felt for that man when he finally came clean bordered on hatred. She'd wanted to hurt him, physically and mentally. Yet despite her anger, she'd had the common sense to realize she was stuck at his cabin until morning. No use risking life and limb to get home.

He'd begged her to take his bed—"I'll sleep on the couch," he'd said, but she hadn't been able to bear the thought of crawling back into the bed where they'd just made love. In the end, she'd gotten her way and curled up on the sofa. Defeated, Aiden had crept back up to the loft.

Lily had been up as soon as the light of the new day filtered through the windows. Having slept in her clothes, all she'd had to do was put on her coat and boots and she'd been ready to head home. When she'd sat up, she'd been startled to see him sitting on the hearth of the fireplace staring ruefully at her. He'd had on jeans and that flannel shirt she'd found so appealing the night before. Only in the morning she'd wanted to rip it off him for another reason. To shred it and throw it into the ashes of the fireplace.

"Got the driveway done," he'd said. "Found a small snow blower in the loft of the garage."

Lily had gotten to her feet. "Then it's time I go."

"You don't even want a coffee? I'd like to talk."

"Nope." She'd found her purse where she'd left it on the bench by the front door and quickly put on her coat and boots.

"At least let me drive your car down to the road for you."

"No thanks." With those words she'd left.

Before beginning her shift, Lily took a bottle of Advil from her desk drawer and popped open the lid. Shaking two extra strengths onto her palm, she downed them with her coffee. Her head pounded. The result of too much wine, too much stress, and not enough sleep.

By midafternoon, Lily needed a break. With a cup of tea and a Danish in hand, she retreated to one of the booths in the back. Her body ached with fatigue and her eyes burned to close. Thankfully, she'd been able to dodge Annie's questions and was grateful when she finally stopped asking what was wrong.

"Mind if I sit down?" came a man's voice from behind her. She knew that voice. She *hated* that voice.

"Sit anywhere you want, except here," she answered without turning to face him.

"Lily, I really need to speak to you. It's important. It's about Sara's murder. I'm here on official business."

So he wasn't going to try to make things right, to apologize yet again. For some reason that hurt.

"Sit."

Aiden took off his jacket and hung it on the coatrack attached to the booth before sliding in opposite her. "I spoke to Philip Kemp this morning. Went over there after you left."

A stab of worry shot through her. Aiden talking to Philip was something she would have liked to have avoided. "And?"

"He told me about seeing you with a gun outside your house and that you had a fight with your sister, but what he claimed happened wouldn't hold up in court. Fact is, the guy hardly saw anything, Lily. I think his imagination ran away with him and, well, he's not the brightest bulb in the chandelier. He jumped the gun. Sorry for the pun." A small smile formed on his lips, but it fell away when she didn't return it. "Anyway, I'm thinking he didn't see what he thought he did, and I really need to know what happened."

Her eyes grew to the size of silver dollars. Did he really want to know her side of the story? Wilkins and Deluca had dismissed her explanation, waving her off and pretty much calling her a liar. She assumed Aiden held the same opinion of her.

Lily sipped her coffee and did her best to give an impression of calm aloofness. Truth was, she wanted more than anything to tell Aiden what happened, especially since he saw the cracks in Philip's version of the events, but she stopped herself before the impulse took hold. How could she trust him after what he'd done to her?

"I've already spoken to Wilkins and Deluca," she said.

"Yeah. I've read your statement and Philip's, as well as the e-mail he sent. Between the two of you, you're the more credible."

She cocked a brow and smirked. "Is this some cop thing you're doing? Trying to get me to think you're on my side so you can gain my trust? 'Cause, buddy, you destroyed that last night."

"No! Lily, *please*. I really am trying to help. Philip Kemp is just some pretty boy and in my opinion, not a credible witness. My gut tells me a lot more went down that day between you and Sara than you're letting on."

He pulled out her typed statement and took a moment, tracing through the lines with a finger, until he came to a stop. "Says here you told the sheriff and his deputy you had a fight with Sara and you did have a gun in your hand, but you never intended to shoot her, but that's all. Why didn't you explain yourself? Why did you have a gun? What were you two fighting about? This is so vague. There are so many unanswered questions." He threw his hands up in a gesture of surrender and looked at her wide-eyed, waiting.

Surprise lit Lily's face. "That's it? That's all that's there?"

Aiden nodded and slid the paper over to her.

She cupped her hands around her mug and let her eyes stray to the sheet. "I said a hell of a lot more than that."

"Tell me what happened then. Tell me *everything*."

CHAPTER 15

Their meeting place was in the parking lot of an abandoned five-pin bowling alley, located in an industrial area out of sight of the main road. The plows had been out during the night, piling mountains of snow around the perimeter of the lot, affording even better cover.

Natalie arrived first, as usual. Antonio was always late. She sipped her cappuccino and turned up the tunes while she waited. Her heart, fueled by caffeine and hatred for Lily Valier, beat like a jackhammer. Every time she thought of either of the Valier sisters, her mind was swept up in a current of anxiety. Sara the slut came dangerously close to ruining her parents' marriage. Even her ghost held power. Natalie had never seen her parents fighting as much as they were now.

Sara might be gone, but her sister Lily remained a thorn in Natalie's side. She knew her type—beautiful and flirty; she could have any man she wanted. Who did that woman think she was fooling, living like a frugal old spinster? Women like Lily made her sick. They used their looks and sexuality to get whatever they wanted. Everything came easy for women like that. Not like for her. She was invisible to men. Never been on a date or had a man other than her dad give her a compliment. Worst of all, Lily Valier made her crave the pills in her pocket. When her worries drifted away, even if for just a few hours, she didn't hate herself as much.

Before going to Antonio for help after Sara's murder, she'd done some digging. It hadn't taken much, just a Google search, and she'd discovered more than enough to know he was a crooked cop. And when he suggested they pin it on Lily, she couldn't have been happier. Yes, she wanted to shout. Yes, yes, yes! That's exactly what I was thinking!

But of course, she let him believe it was all his idea. Men and their egos. It may be a stereotype, but it was one she thought held some truth.

Natalie had thought all night about what she'd tell Antonio to get him back on the scent of Lily's trail. He probably wouldn't buy her story, but she was prepared for that. They'd have a little to and fro, their usual game. She'd be the earnest teenager just trying to help and he the big, brave cop whose job it was to be suspicious of her story. It didn't matter either way. They were playing their parts; they both knew it and in the end, he'd listen to her.

The pounding in her chest was uncomfortable now, driving her to feel around in her jacket for the pill bottle. One little pill and her nerves would soon be calmed. With expert fingers, she one-handedly popped the bottle open, shook one out, and downed it with her cappuccino.

Natalie didn't see Antonio at first, but when she caught movement in the edge of her eye, she clicked off the radio and rolled down the window.

"Mornin'," Deputy Deluca said from his own car, which he'd parked alongside Natalie's SUV in the opposite direction so they'd be face-to-face when the windows were down. His hangdog face twitched up briefly into a smile. "What's so important we had to meet in person?"

She thought about the envelope of crisp hundred-dollar bills she'd placed in her glove compartment. The ones she planned on handing over to this all-too-willing crooked cop. Now how could she do that over the phone?

She smirked. "Sometimes it's just nice to see your face."

Antonio cocked his head, returning the smirk. "It may be my day off, but I've got a crap load of paperwork waiting for me at the office, and I already told you everything I know about the Sara Valier investigation."

The deputy wasn't the kind of man to be working on his day off, but Natalie pretended to buy his story. "I won't keep you long then. But why not give this some thought... *I* might have something important to tell *you*?" She saluted him with her Styrofoam cup.

He laughed. "Yeah? You gonna break the case wide open for me?"

"What if I told you I know where the gun is? The one Lily shot her sister with?"

Antonio's jaw fell open wider than Natalie had thought humanly possible. She could have counted his fillings if she was so inclined.

Deluca's eyes narrowed. "Now how the hell would you know that?" he said, using his best cop voice.

"Don't go getting all *official* on me. I'm not saying I have the gun or my dad has it. But I do know who does and exactly where you can find it."

"No, you don't." The words came slowly, as if he were daring Natalie to convince him.

She smiled widely. "Oh, yes I do! And if you want me to tell you, you'd better be nice."

She leaned over and opened the glove compartment, snagging the envelope of cash. "First, this is for the info you gave me the other day, and you know there's more to come if you keep me in the loop. Now, when I tell you about the gun and where you can find it, you sure as hell better promise to let me know everything about the investigation, *and* I don't want you questioning my dad about the murder again, OK?"

Antonio snatched the envelope like it was a raw steak held over the head of a hungry crocodile. "I smell something fishy."

She had half a mind to drive off. "You're not being nice."

"OK, OK. I'm sorry. Where's the gun?"

"In the Higgstown Diner. Under the couch in Lily's office but not in plain sight. It's under the rug."

He laughed. "And you know this how?"

"I heard Lily say it herself yesterday. That's why I wanted to meet with you. She was telling one of the waitresses. Annie I think her name is. They're kinda friendly and I guess she needed someone to spill to. She was crying when she told her. I'd get there quick if I were you, Deluca. I think she was trying to figure out a way to get rid of it once and for all."

He frowned. "Come on. You think I was born yesterday?"

"Does it really matter? It was your idea to pin the murder on Lily, or did you forget about your big payday once she's arrested?"

He was silent for a moment, then grinned and tipped his head to her. "I'll need something in writing."

"I'm willing to make an official statement, but it has to be anonymous."

"Good enough. But you're sure it'll be there? I don't want to look like a fool."

Natalie held a hand over her heart. "I swear on my mother's grave."

"Your mother's not dead."

Natalie laughed. The pill had her now.

"All right, but it'll take a day or so to get the warrant. I'll meet you at the station to get that statement." With that, he rolled up his window and spun the car around. It fishtailed on the hardened snow as he made his way out of the parking lot with Natalie Lyons following behind.

A grateful little smile unfolded on her lips. At least she'd have some time to figure out how the hell she was gonna get that gun into Lily's office.

CHAPTER 16

"We weren't really fighting, you know. Sara and I, I mean. It was more like a battle of wills. I had a gun, yes, I won't deny that, but I wasn't *aiming* it at her. I was holding it out, handle first, trying to get her to take it with her."

"Really?"

She wasn't sure of his tone, but his eyes told her something. He was watching intently like any good cop, looking for signs of innocence or guilt. If that was what he wanted—the truth—then she would be more than happy to give it to him. He'd know it when he saw it and that gave her comfort.

Annie approached the table with a pot of coffee. "Would you like some, Aiden? More for you, Lily?"

Lily pushed her cup toward Annie, frustrated by her bad timing. She was just getting into the meat of the story, *her* story. The one she'd been longing to tell someone who was willing to listen. Though she didn't fully trust Aiden, he was still her best chance at clearing her name and maybe even finding Sara's killer. So she swallowed the animosity she was still feeling toward him.

Annie filled Lily's mug, then looked to Aiden for his reply.

"Sure thing, Annie. I'd love a cup."

A huge smile spread across Annie's face as she filled his mug to almost overflowing, stopping just before it spilled onto the table.

"Thanks," Lily said dismissively, sending Annie scurrying off. "Look, I already told you how Zander threatened Sara's baby."

Aiden ripped open a packet of sugar and emptied it into his coffee, stirring. "But she didn't seem scared enough to take the gun. You argued over it, right?"

"Sara thought I was overreacting and said I just didn't know Zander well enough, and that he'd never hurt her or their baby." Lily sighed. "Where are you going with this?"

Aiden grinned. "Right now, I'm just on a fact-finding mission. What you've told me fits well with Philip Kemp's version, only he didn't have the luxury of actually hearing any of the conversation between you and Sara. But there's something nagging at me." He sipped his coffee. "Zander's a married man with a grown daughter, and if his wife found out about the affair and pregnancy, I imagine she wouldn't be happy about it. It would complicate matters, wouldn't it? I mean, Zander Lyons is a wealthy man."

Aiden's statement hung heavily in the air. The baby would have been an heir, an heir not just to Zander's fortune, but to Sara's as well. Was he feeling her out?

Wanting to see how she'd react? If she'd mention the money? It always came down to the damned money. Any way you sliced it, all those millions were right there in the middle of things.

"I never wanted the money, Mr. O'Rourke. I made it clear to my sister she could keep it all. She offered me half, you know. She wasn't a selfish woman. I told her if she wanted to give me something then let me have the diner."

His brows lifted, but she was unsure of his expression. Was he surprised Sara offered her half of the money or that she called him Mr. O'Rourke?

Then she remembered something. Something she hadn't the heart to tell her sister. "Zander came here, to the diner. He sat right over there." Lily pointed to the largest booth in the restaurant, the one big enough to seat eight. "He was alone. I walked up to him, smiling, but he glared back at me. I tried to start a conversation, telling him what I was sure he already knew, that I was Sara's sister, and even held out my hand. He left me hanging, sneering as if I was something dirty he didn't dare touch. For Sara's sake, I ignored his rudeness and asked what he'd like to order.

"He told me he wasn't here to eat and that I shouldn't put ideas into my sister's head. Then he said something I'll never forget. I remember his exact words. 'She's having that abortion even if I have to do it myself.' He ordered a coffee, left it untouched, threw a fifty-dollar bill on the table and left. Maybe if Sara knew what he'd said, she would have been more careful. She might have even wanted to take the gun."

Aiden stared at her for a moment, then leaned back, spreading his arms across the back of the booth. His eyes narrowed and he tilted his head, making him look exactly like what he was—a hard-boiled, cynical detective. What was he up to, some cop trick? Waiting for her to continue, to maybe say something incriminating? She felt her insides drop with disappointment.

He didn't believe her.

She shook her head, then stood and peered down at him. "You son of a bitch. I loved my sister more than anyone in the world. I would never hurt her. Never!" With hands planted on her hips, she yelled, "Get the hell out of here. I'm done with you. I thought you wanted the truth and that's what I gave you."

A smile played on his lips as he looked up at her.

"Why the hell are you smiling?"

"Because I believe you. It makes sense. Things are falling into place. And, well, I'm glad."

"Glad?"

He sighed. "I'm sorry if I upset you. That wasn't my intention. It's my job to ask questions and to be suspicious of everyone, but to be honest, I never wanted you to be a suspect."

Anger still burned in her, but she sat back down. Was he being sincere or just shoveling cop bullshit at her to lull her into a false sense of security? She crossed her arms tightly over her chest and pressed her lips into a thin line of displeasure.

"I believe you," he said again, adding a measure of emphasis to his tone, "but we've got more to talk about. Like where the gun is now. Do you have any idea what might have happened to it?"

Lily stiffened.

Aiden seemed to catch the movement, or rather, the lack of it. "What? What's wrong?"

She turned away, not wanting to answer.

He splayed both hands on the Arborite and pushed himself to standing. "I can't bloody well help you if you don't talk to me. I know you're still upset about last night and I'm sorry. I was an idiot. I made a mistake, but I need your help. Do you, or do you not want your sister's murderer found?"

His anger startled her. It was a side of him she hadn't yet seen. But if the murder weapon was found and it was her gun, Wilkins and Deluca would have the evidence they needed to arrest her. "I don't know where it is, and I'm not sure I want it found." Her voice was almost a whisper. "If the bullets that killed my sister came from my gun, they'll charge me. The gun was registered. It'd be easy to match the slugs to the weapon. Even I know that and I'm no cop."

"Not unless it has Zander's fingerprints on it. We've got to find that gun."

Lily's heart beat hard against her ribs. Was he right? Could it be a good thing to find the gun? "What if it was wiped clean? Then I'd still be a suspect."

"It's a chance I'm willing to take, Lily."

Sure, it was easy for him to gamble with her life, but was it a chance she was willing to take? "Like I said, I have no idea where it is."

He nodded and chewed on his lower lip. "OK. Then we have to find it." He flipped through his notes and looked up. "They tested you for gunpowder residue when you were first brought in for questioning and you came up clean, right? That's a very good thing you've got working in your favor. Don't be afraid." He sounded so much like a detective now, so distant and businesslike.

"Think it may be time to pay a visit to the Lyons household." Aiden stood and gathered up his notes. "Thank you for your time, Miss Valier."

CHAPTER 17

The woman heading down the black-and-white staircase had her eyes glued to him. She was beautiful in a past-her-prime sort of way. The kind of woman some men might call a cougar, and the way she was eyeing him made Aiden feel like he was prey.

"You can go now, Sabina," Gabrielle Lyons told her housekeeper without looking at her.

"Sorry for the unexpected visit, ma'am. My name's Aiden O'Rourke." He held out his hand, and she held on a bit too long for his liking. She looked him over from head to toe, then back up again, making him feel like he was about to be devoured.

"Lovely to meet you, Mr. O'Rourke, I'm Gabrielle Lyons. What can I do for you?" Her voice was lined in silk.

"I'm a private investigator, ma'am, working on the Sara Valier murder, and I was wondering if your husband was around. I'd like to talk to him. Promise I won't take too much of his time. I know he's a busy man."

The woman crossed her arms tightly over her chest. "What would make you think Zander would be home at this time of day? He's at work." Her tone had become icy. "Besides, he's already spoken to Deputy Deluca and was cleared as a suspect. He wasn't even in town when that Sara woman was killed."

Aiden smiled inwardly. He knew damn well Zander wouldn't be home during the day. What he really wanted was to meet his lovely missus and pop by Zander's fancy office right after. After all, Gabrielle Lyons had a reason to want Sara dead too.

"Where was he the night Miss Valier was shot? Do you happen to remember?" Aiden asked.

"On a business trip. In Canada…Toronto, I think."

"I'd like to see something concrete that puts him there. Like a hotel receipt. Do you know if he has anything like that?"

Gabrielle's eyes flashed with anger for a second, and her lips parted as if she was about to say something. Instead, she smiled. "I wouldn't have the faintest idea where Zander would keep something like that. All I know is the deputy investigated his alibi, and my husband was cleared." She reached out and touched his shoulder. "Why don't you come on in for a coffee. I'll call Zander at the office and tell him to come home."

It was his lucky day. Speaking to Zander Lyons at home would be much easier than trying to get past security in his office building, a task he was dreading.

"That sounds great." Aiden stepped forward off the rug at the door and onto the marble.

"Please remove your boots. Lots of snow out there and I wouldn't want you dirtying up my clean floors." Gabrielle laughed, but Aiden noted it was without humor.

The kitchen was huge, the size of his entire cabin. The echoing of their voices bouncing off the granite, marble, and hardwood was unsettling.

Gabrielle gestured to the tall, upholstered stools lined up on one side of a granite counter top. Aiden took a seat. She stood on the opposite side of the counter and leaned seductively over it, her blouse falling open to reveal red lace.

"Sabina!" Gabrielle called. A moment later, her housekeeper, a stout Italian-looking woman, was back, standing at attention like a robot awaiting an order. "A fresh pot of coffee. Use the percolator, not that crappy coffee maker Zander likes. Oh, and bring in the tray of cupcakes. I think you left it in the prep kitchen." She turned back to Aiden. He'd left his jacket on a bench by the front door, and her eyes now wandered over his arms and chest. One hand lay restlessly on the counter so close to his arm he could feel her body heat.

Gabrielle bit her bottom lip and looked up coyly. Aiden was rarely scared, but this woman was making him wish he had a shot of whisky to down. An awkward silence stretched between them like a small forever until finally, he spoke. "Thought you were going to call your husband."

Without taking her eyes from him, she picked up the cordless from the counter and punched in a number.

The housekeeper was back, carrying a silver, three-tiered tray filled with cupcakes of various colors. She set it down between Aiden and Gabrielle.

Gabrielle plucked up a red one. Red velvet, he guessed, knowing how popular they were lately, though he'd never had one. She peeled off the wrapper, cradling the phone between ear and shoulder. Daintily, she licked the creamy frosting from the top and then took a nibble. With a sigh, she put the cupcake down. "Zander, come home right now. It's important." There was a pause and she said, "Because there's someone here to see you." Another pause. "You'll find out when you get here." She hung up and resumed her love affair with the tiny red cake.

CHAPTER 18

With only an hour left until closing, Lily decided to call it a day.

"Annie?" she called to her friend, who was busy polishing the counter top and straightening the menus.

"Yeah?" Annie answered without looking up.

"I'm gonna go now. Will you lock up?"

"Yup." Her tone was stony.

Lily placed a hand on her arm. "Sorry about how I spoke to you when Aiden was here. I didn't mean it. He and I, well, we're not on the best of terms right now."

Annie turned to the grill and began scraping it clean. "No need to explain."

"He's a detective. Wilkins hired him," she said.

Annie threw down the scraper and turned to face Lily, her mouth agape. "What?"

"It's true. He was only trying to get close to me to see if I killed my sister."

"Oh, Lil, I'm so sorry. I don't know what to say." She walked around to the other side of the counter, and for a moment Lily thought she was going to hug her. She might have liked a hug at that moment, but Annie stopped herself and instead gave her a sympathetic frown.

"There's nothing to say. It is what it is. At any rate, I told him everything and I think he believes me and wants to help, so things are looking up." She tried to inject a cheery tone into her voice.

"Hon, are you OK? Is there anything I can do?"

Lily had had no time to assess her emotions. How *did* she feel? That was an excellent question. In the short time she'd known Aiden, or thought she knew him, he'd stolen a large piece of her heart, but he'd betrayed her in the worst way possible. What hurt most was knowing she'd been his number one suspect. How could she ever trust him again?

"I'm fine, Annie." She sighed at the heavy realization of the falseness of her words. She needed to go before the tears started. "Gonna duck out now, OK?"

Annie nodded and smiled. "Sure thing, girlfriend. Got it all under control."

* * *

"Wilkins in?" Lily asked after pulling open the front doors of the sheriff's department.

Julia, the shortest, fattest deputy in the East, was seated behind the counter. She eyed Lily with contempt like everyone else in town.

"He's busy."

"So, that means he's in." Lily kept walking, right past deputy fat ass and straight to Wilkins's office. A halfhearted "Hey" came from behind her but no approaching footfalls. Probably too lazy to get off her ass.

"You son of a—"

Wilkins was on his feet in a flash, stilling Lily with two words, "Aiden O'Rourke."

She huffed in frustration. "Why?"

"It's not personal, Lily. You know that. Just doin' my job." Wilkins sat down and gestured for Lily to do the same.

She stepped farther into his office but didn't sit. "No. You're doing nothing. You hired Aiden to do your job."

Wilkins pulled open a drawer and took out a bottle of Pepto-Bismol, unscrewed the top and took a swig, then put the lid back on and put it back. "All this crap is giving me an ulcer." He pounded a fist on his blotter. "Damn, I can't believe he's blown his cover so early. Maybe it was a mistake to bring him in."

She hadn't expected this reaction. Her intentions were to blast Wilkins, let him know she was onto his game and then leave, but now, a knot of worry tightened in her gut. Was Wilkins going to fire Aiden now, after he'd given her a small glimmer of hope and told her he believed her?

"I have nothing to hide. I didn't kill my sister! Let him finish his goddamn investigation."

Fire blazed in the sheriff's dark eyes. "Calm yourself. Why don't I have Julia bring you a cup of tea, and we can talk about this. Sit down." Wilkins's voice was deep with authority.

She didn't want to stay another second. Her heart pounded with fear. What had she done? Was Aiden going to be sent packing? And why was she so scared he might be? Because he promised to help find her sister's killer, or was there more to it than that?

Lily finally sat with an indelicate drop into the creaky old chair. Wilkins buzzed Julia and a moment later, a cup of hot water and a tea bag were placed in front of her. Julia slapped a couple of sugar packets down beside it and left.

"Should I call my lawyer?" Lily asked.

"No need for that." Wilkins gave his head a good shake. "Look, this is as frustrating for me as it is for you. As much as I want to, I can't clear you as a suspect yet, Lily."

"So, Aiden will continue with the investigation?"

He sighed, deep and long. "Suppose so. Guess it's best to let the man do his job."

"Was he expensive?"

"Beg your pardon?"

"Just wondering how much you paid to try to bring the dangerous criminal, Lily Valier, to justice."

A voice came from behind her. "You could save us some dough if you confessed." It was Deluca.

She was on her feet, her tea untouched. She looked at Wilkins. "Why don't you save the taxpayers some money and retire? You're getting a wage for sitting on your ass doing nothing but harassing innocent women."

Deluca made his way to her side and touched her arm, but Lily pulled away. He grinned and took a step back. "I understand how frustrating this must be for you, but you're the most likely suspect at the moment."

"Really? I'd think Zander or Gabrielle Lyons would be higher up on your list. My sister was pregnant with Zander's child. He wanted her to have an abortion, and when she refused, he threatened the life of her child."

"You've already told us that, Miss Valier, and Zander Lyons vehemently denies the accusation and besides, he has an alibi."

"What about Gabrielle then? Was she even brought in for questioning?"

"We spoke to Mrs. Lyons and, frankly, she really doesn't fit the profile."

"You've got to be kidding me! Profile? What profile? It's not like you're hunting down a terrorist here. She's the wife of a philandering husband, one who happened to impregnate my sister. Isn't that enough of a motive?" She wanted to scream, stamp her feet, pull out her hair.

Deluca shook his head and gave Lily a condescending look. "No, I'm sorry, but we really don't think she's guilty of the crime. And before you even bring up his name, Phil Kemp is an even less likely suspect, so, guess who that leaves?" Deluca's grin was now a wide smile.

Lily looked at the sheriff with pleading eyes. "Why are you letting him take over this case?"

The sheriff ran a hand over his closely cropped gray hair. "I'm not letting him take over, but Deputy Deluca does have experience with homicides."

Deluca broke in, "Don't forget we've got a third party involved now. It was Sheriff Wilkins's idea to get some extra help, so I haven't actually taken anything over. I'd say Aiden has done that."

Lily wanted to say so much more. She wanted to call them both a few choice names but said only, "You know where you can put that cup of tea, don't ya?" before turning on her heel and stomping from the office.

CHAPTER 19

The sound of a door opening caught Aiden's attention. Zander must have run a few red lights to get home so quickly, but he was grateful for the added company. Gabrielle was on her second cupcake, this time a chocolate one. Maybe she'd behave herself with her husband in the room.

"Hey," came a female voice.

"Oh, hi, honey," Gabrielle answered stiffly, the word "honey" seeming to stick in her throat. "This is Aiden. He's a private dick, here to ask your dear old daddy some questions." She plucked up a cake and held it out. "Want one?" She threw her daughter a wink.

The girl shook her head. "Surprised you're willing to share."

"This is my loving daughter, Natalie," Gabrielle said to Aiden with a nonchalant wave of her hand.

Natalie gave a nod in his direction, narrowed her eyes, and skulked out of the room.

A cup of coffee and another cupcake later, Zander Lyons finally made his entrance. Aiden stood and offered a hand in greeting. The tall man swung his briefcase onto the counter, making his wife jump. "Who the hell are you?"

"Aiden O'Rourke. I'm a private investigator. Sheriff Wilkins brought me in to help with the Sara Valier murder investigation."

Zander gave Aiden's hand a reluctant shake then turned to his wife. "Why don't you and your cupcakes disappear and let me talk to Mr. O'Rourke in private."

Gabrielle let out a huff of displeasure before leaving.

"This is why I was summoned?" Zander said, anger coloring his voice.

"I won't take much of your time."

"Hope not."

Aiden wondered if he should sit down again or whether they were going to have the entire conversation standing up. He decided to let Zander take the lead and if he sat, Aiden would follow suit.

Zander stood like a statue, legs slightly apart, arms folded tightly across his chest, the seams of his expensive suit jacket straining.

"I'll get right to the point, Mr. Lyons. According to your statement, you empathically deny having anything to do with Sara Valier's murder. You do, however, admit she was carrying your child and you were not happy about that. Is that correct?"

Zander's lips tightened into a grim mask of displeasure. "I did not want another child. That's correct.

Look, do I need a lawyer?" He plucked his cell phone from his pocket, finger poised over the keypad.

Aiden smiled in an attempt to disarm him. "No. Not at all. I'm just coming in late in the game and have to play catch-up. No need for lawyers."

Zander cocked a thick brow, studying him, then seemingly satisfied, put the phone away. "Hurry and ask your questions. I have work to do."

"Did you ask Miss Valier to have an abortion?"

"Yes. I told her I would take care of everything…all the expenses."

"Did she want to keep the baby?"

There was a moment of hesitation before he answered, "No. We were in agreement that she'd…take care of things."

"Really?" Aiden asked, then waved him off. "It's OK, no need to answer that. I understand you were out of town on business the day of the murder. I'd like to see some proof, a receipt or credit card statement. Do you have anything like that?"

"You're not a cop. I don't have to prove anything to you. I already spoke to the authorities about that."

The man was right. He had no authority to demand such a thing, but sometimes he got lucky. Suspects panicked and said and did things their lawyers would have fits over.

"OK. One last thing and I'll leave you alone. What do you know about firearms? Do you own any and, if so, are you experienced in their use?" Aiden noticed Zander's expression change from one of anger to uncertainty. He knew the look of a man who was about to lie.

"Absolutely not."

* * *

No one saw Natalie leave, a satchel casually slung across her shoulder.

She made it to the diner with only half an hour to spare before closing and sat in the booth at the back. After shrugging off the bag, she eyed the restaurant carefully, taking note of who was where and what they were doing. Annie was at the front, cashing out some old guy. A group of teenagers sat by the window, and a middle-aged man, draining a coffee mug, was engrossed in the news on the flat screen over the counter. Other than that, no one else was there.

The only worry she had was that Lily was in the back somewhere. Natalie twisted around to look down the short hallway. Lights were off. That was a good sign. She decided to make her move before Annie spotted her and came for her order.

She was on her feet and moved as fast as she could without breaking into a run. It had been years since she'd wandered to the back of the diner looking for the washroom, but she remembered the layout. In particular Lily's office because the walls were covered with pictures of the Valier family.

So many photos all in the same black frames. They'd piqued her curiosity and lured her in. Most were of Lily and her sister, Sara, the home wrecker, at various ages. A few of their mother Nancy too. In all of them, Lily and Sara looked deliriously happy, with their arms around each other, smiles huge and genuine. She remembered one picture in particular—the girls just freckle-faced kids, in summer at the beach, their mother looking on, watching them play. A real mother, one who loved them and would do anything for them. Even without a dad they were a happy family. Her heart broke at the sight of them, and her hatred, borne of jealousy, grew even more.

Natalie made her way past the staff room to Lily's office. If she was discovered, she'd say she was looking for the washroom.

The room was black as pitch, making Natalie stop in her tracks for fear of accidentally knocking something over. She dared not turn on the light. Luckily she'd thought of everything. Natalie was nothing if not conscientious and resourceful. She fished out her cell phone from her jacket pocket. Its feeble light was enough. She shone it around the room and finally let out the breath she'd been holding. It was the same! *Exactly* the same.

The room was small and Natalie was by the couch in just three strides. She pulled out a pair of leather gloves from her bag and put them on, then lay down on the worn area rug that covered most of the floor. She could smell the old of the place, the dust in the rug, the worn wooden floorboards and the leather of the couch. Reaching out, she shoved her arm and shoulder as far as possible under it. The wood frame pressed into the flesh of her upper arm despite the down fill of her winter jacket, but the pain was worth it. Finally, her fingers reached the end of the rug. She could feel the fringe on it, stiff and ragged with age. She plucked it up and with her other hand, removed the gun from her satchel and placed it underneath the carpet in the farthest corner. Exactly where she'd told Antonio he could find it.

CHAPTER 20

Lily's world had turned on a dime. Yesterday, she didn't have much, but she did have a ray of hope thanks to Aiden. When she got to work that morning, disaster was waiting in the form of Wilkins and Deluca.

Cell phone in hand, she was about to do the unthinkable—call Aiden. What choice did she have? The sheriff and his deputy were there, in her diner, in her office with a search warrant.

"Go ahead," she'd said when Deluca handed the warrant over. "You won't find anything." She *knew* that was the truth. But unbelievably, they had found something.

Deputy Deluca headed straight to her old leather couch and pulled it away from the wall in one heavy-handed heft, and there it was. A bulge under the carpet. She had no idea what "it" was, but panic swelled her throat.

In the moment before Deluca whipped back the carpet, it came to her with absolute certainty what that bulge was. It was her gun. What scared her most was how on earth it had gotten there.

With the weapon bagged, Wilkins stood in front of Lily and dangled it. She could see it through the plastic. The pearl-handled gun that had been her mother's.

"Can you identify this?"

Lily was too stunned to answer.

"Is this yours?" Wilkins said again, pulling her from her stupor.

She felt her head moving, nodding yes as if an invisible puppeteer controlled her. In her mind, she screamed, No. Stop. Don't admit to anything.

Wilkins turned away. "Antonio, make a note that Ms. Valier has admitted this is her gun." He faced her again. "We'll have the ballistics report back by this afternoon. I strongly suggest you stay in town." Then, before leaving, he asked, "Is there anything you want to tell me?"

This time she had the good sense not to answer.

* * *

Aiden knew immediately from the wobble in Lily's voice something wasn't right. "What's wrong?"

"They found it," she said in a voice devoid of hope.

"Who found what?"

"Wilkins and Deluca came to the diner with a warrant. They found my gun. Only…"

"At the diner?" A million things ran through his head. Why the hell hadn't she told him she had the gun? Then again, if he knew what would he have done about it? Help her to get rid of it or turn it in to Wilkins?

Aiden realized she hadn't finished her sentence and hoped it wasn't more bad news. "Only what?"

A shuddering sigh came from the other end of the line. "Only, I don't know how it got here. It was in my office under the rug. I didn't put it there. Please, Aiden, *please* believe me."

The desperation in her voice brought something out in him he hadn't expected. He wanted to hold Lily in his arms and reassure her everything would be fine. That he would take care of her. Something very close to fear edged in on him then. What if he couldn't help her?

After some thought, fear was replaced by fury. Where had all this come from? He knew nothing about a warrant. Wilkins hadn't told him a thing. Why was he being kept out of the loop?

"I'll come as soon as I can, but first, I have to find out what's going on. Don't go anywhere. Wait for me, OK?"

It didn't take long for Aiden to find Deluca at the station. "Mind filling me in on what's going on with Lily Valier?" he demanded when he spotted the deputy.

Deluca smiled his twitchy little smile, but his eyes were lit up. "You're just the hired help," he said. "We've got all we need now. As soon as we get confirmation Lily's gun is the murder weapon, you'll get paid and you can get the hell out of town."

Aiden's hands fisted at his sides. "How did you find out about the gun?"

"Good old-fashioned police work," Deluca said, a grin in his voice.

Aiden wasn't buying what he was selling. His gut told him Lily was being framed. "She didn't do it, Deluca. You've got it all wrong. I spoke to Zander Lyons and his charming wife yesterday. That's who you should be shining a big-ass spotlight on. By the way, I'd like to have a look at the proof Zander provided you with. You know, his alibi for the night of the murder."

Deluca laughed. "Maybe it's time you go back to the big city." He turned to walk away, but Aiden planted a hand on his shoulder.

The deputy looked down at it and then his gaze rose to Aiden's eyes, but Aiden didn't move his hand. He held the small man in place and spoke again, "I'm not finished. You hired me to do a job—"

"Wilkins hired you. I told him we didn't need the help. Just a waste of department money." Deluca pulled away and Aiden let him go, but followed him to his office.

Once there, Deluca picked up the receiver of his desk phone. "As a matter of fact, I'm so confident we'll get a match on the gun, I'm gonna get Julia to write up that check for you now. That way you'll beat the traffic on your way back home. I'm sure Wilkins won't mind."

"Don't bother. I don't want your money."

Deluca replaced the receiver and sat in his chair. "Well then, thanks for the work you did for us. Call if you need a recommendation. Hope all that snow won't make your drive out of town too hellish." His smile was wide, and Aiden noticed for the first time how small his teeth were.

Aiden's eyes narrowed. He turned to Wilkins's office but found it empty. He went to the reception area looking for Julia.

"Where's the sheriff?" Aiden asked when he spied her hunched over the front desk.

She looked up from her crossword puzzle. "Gone to Bangor. He took the evidence up there himself."

"By evidence, I suppose you're referring to the gun that was planted in Lily Valier's office?"

Julia's eyes widened and her jaw fell open just a little. "Planted?" Her voice dimmed to a whisper.

Aiden nodded. "Why did he take it himself?"

"He's waiting for the report personally. Wants the results as soon as he can get 'em."

Time was running out for Lily Valier.

CHAPTER 21

Despite the excitement, or perhaps because of it, the diner was packed. Having the sheriff and deputy show up with flashers on and toting a search warrant, signaling they were on official business, kept the patrons' butts in their seats a bit longer than usual. Cell phones were yanked out of pockets, and soon word spread. Then it was standing room only at the Higgstown Diner.

As tempting as it was to turn the "Open" sign to "Closed," Lily decided to keep the place open. What signal would closing up send? It would be an admission of guilt. No, she decided, she was going to hold her head high. She had nothing to be ashamed of or feel guilty about.

Lily was at the back of the restaurant, standing at the entrance to the hallway, when she saw Aiden in the doorway, broad shoulders blotting out the hazy autumn light behind him.

Soon, he was at her side. Strong, gentle hands rested on her shoulders. "Are you OK?"

She caught herself breathing in the scent of him—the outdoors, soap, and a hint of cologne. "No. Not really." The warmth of tears gathered behind her eyes.

"Can you pack up quickly? I can take you home to pick up some stuff."

His words not only baffled her but scared her too. Why would he want her to pack up? Was he here to collect her and bring her to the sheriff? "Why?" Lily choked out.

"Because you're coming with me to the cabin."

"What?" It didn't make sense. That's the last place in the world she wanted to see again. She turned away from him, trying to find something to do, busywork to take her mind off her troubles.

She cleared off a table and walked away, arms filled with dirty dishes. He followed her to the kitchen, waiting expectantly for a response. Lily put the dishes into a plastic tub with a clatter.

"Did you hear what I just said?" he asked.

"I heard you, but I don't understand what the hell you're trying to do, Aiden. What would going to your cabin accomplish?"

He spoke slowly, but sternly. "They're going to arrest you."

The tears she'd been trying to hold back finally fell hotly down her cheeks, and she wiped them away with her apron.

"You have to come with me, Lily. Give me a chance to help you, please."

She huffed her displeasure. "How do I know you're not helping them? I don't trust you as far as I could bloody well throw you. Go home and I mean your *real* home. Go back to Chicago, if that's where you're really from."

He reached out and tried to pull her into an embrace. She pummeled his chest, but he wouldn't let go, pulling her closer until finally she let herself be held. She was crying now, sobbing into his shoulder.

"I'm not the enemy. I'm going to do everything in my power to keep you safe, but we have to move quickly." He held her at arm's length and looked her in the eyes. "Lily, trust me. I won't betray you again."

Confusion reigned. She wanted to trust him, yet she didn't want to run. She was too tired for running.

"They'll figure out I'm with you. Wilkins and Deluca will just come to the cabin to arrest me," she said, shaking her head.

"I won't let them in. They'll have to get a warrant. It'll buy us some time."

She ran her hands through her hair, and it took everything she had not to pull it out in frustration. "Time for what?"

Aiden bent to her level and grabbed her shoulders. "To find the real killer."

"You're not making sense! There's no use, Aiden. I might as well turn myself in. They're coming to get me, and you can't do anything about it." She left him, made her way into the dining area, and looked around at the place she loved most in the world. She thought of late-night talks with her mother and sister, the three of them comfy in their pajamas, sharing a big bowl of popcorn, laughing. In those moments, she felt anything was possible. That life was good, that she was safe and her future was bright.

When she was older, her memories were of her mother waiting tables and Sara at the grill. Lily's job was cleaning up, a bottom-of-the-totem-pole position. But she never complained because she was in the bosom of her family, a family she hadn't expected to lose so quickly and tragically.

Soon she'd be leaving it all behind. Lily walked to what used to be their booth—hers and Aiden's—with Aiden a step behind. An elderly man looked up from his coffee cup, one substantial gray eyebrow cocked as if to say: What the heck do you want?

Only he didn't have to ask. Lily spoke before he had the chance. "Gerry, any chance I can sit here with my friend for just a bit?"

Gerry nodded furiously, his mouth full of the last of his coffee. He scooped up his newspaper and made his way to the register to pay.

"No need, Ger. It's on the house today," Lily called after him.

Too much was going on inside her head, and she wanted desperately to shut off her thoughts. Her stomach twisted with anxiety, and her mind churned with worry. What would happen to her beloved diner when she went to prison? Where would Rex go? And to complicate matters more, what just happened between her and Aiden? He'd hugged her; she'd let him, but what were they to each other? Should she dare put her faith in his words that he'd find the real killer? Or was he going to leave as soon as Wilkins and Deluca came for her?

"It's got to be Zander Lyons or maybe even his wife. I don't understand why they're not taking a harder look at that family," Aiden said, breaking into her thoughts.

Lily folded her arms over her chest and sighed. "No more. I can't talk about this now."

"What? Why?"

"Because I want to take in what's left of my freedom."

Aiden was quiet for a moment, then with a frown said, "OK." He reached a hand across the table, obviously wanting her to take hold of it, but she turned away and he slid it back to his side. "Sorry."

"Do me one favor?" There was a hitch in her voice.

"Anything."

"If they do arrest me, find someone to take care of Rex. Maybe Annie would do it. Yes, I think she might. She loves him."

"I'll take care of him."

She threw him a puzzled look.

"I'm staying in Higgstown until I can prove your innocence. I won't rest until I find who killed your sister."

She nodded and smiled, though it was perfunctory. "All right, but if you change your mind—"

"I won't."

Her thoughts turned to her friends at the Evelyn Harrison Seniors Center, especially Mrs. G., and her heart shattered. She'd never see them again, and what would they think when they found out she'd been arrested?

Through the din and clatter of the diner, she heard a cell phone ring. It was Aiden's. He fished it from his jacket pocket and looked at the screen. "It's Wilkins," he said before answering.

Her eyes grew wide and her heart beat triple time, but she said nothing.

He hit talk and plugged his ear with a finger so he could hear over the commotion. "What do you want?" he said loudly.

Lily barely heard Wilkins's familiar voice through Aiden's phone but couldn't make out what he was saying.

"Yeah, I'm still in town. I told you I wasn't going anywhere."

Aiden nodded a few times, then smiled the biggest smile she'd ever seen.

"I'll let her know. She's right in front of me." He ended the call, returned the phone to his pocket, then got to his feet, pulling her with him. After planting a big kiss on her forehead, he said, "Turns out you're not going to be arrested after all."

CHAPTER 22

"We can't make the arrest," Deputy Deluca said.

"What?" Natalie screamed into the phone. "Thanks to me, you got what you needed! What more do you imbeciles have to have in order to arrest that woman?"

"The ballistics report was a match, but the prints on the gun weren't Lily's. The lab got a good set of fingerprints as well as a palm print. We'd already tested Lily Valier for powder residue when we brought her in for questioning and she'd come up clean. There's no way she fired that gun."

"Shit, shit, shit," Natalie mumbled as she paced her room, a hand entwined in her hair, pulling. She'd been careful not to get any prints on the gun when she planted it, and even wiped it down before hiding it under her bed. There was no way they'd gotten a print. He was lying, trying to frighten her, but why? Maybe they'd planted evidence. Could they have put her dad's prints on the gun out of desperation just to close the case?

"But you said the bullets matched the gun and the gun was Lily's," she whined, trying not to cry.

"Doesn't matter. We found prints, and like I said, they weren't Lily's." Antonio's voice rose this time, driving home the point.

"Fix it! What do I pay you for?" Natalie yelled. Of course she couldn't say what she wanted to, that she knew there couldn't possibly be prints on the gun.

"No matter how much money you throw at me, I can't do a damn thing about this. Wilkins brought the gun to the lab himself and waited for the report."

"But I thought—"

"What? That having me in your back pocket would keep your dad out of prison? That I could make all your family troubles go away?"

"I could tell on you. What do you think would happen if I told Sheriff Wilkins I was paying you off?" Her voice held a lilt, a singsongy threat, like a taunting kid on the playground.

Antonio laughed. "You can't prove a damn thing. Go ahead and tell, Natalie. You want a surefire way to make your dad look guilty? 'Cause telling my boss you're paying me to keep him out of jail will make it seem like you know something we don't. Maybe you're obstructing justice. You'll go to prison too."

Her throat cinched. Antonio was right. She knew if Lily was in the clear, they'd have no choice but to come for her dad, and what if the prints were his? His alibi was flimsy. Had Deluca double-crossed her?

Antonio heaved a sigh. She pictured him sitting slumped in his car, probably in some doughnut shop parking lot slurping coffee and stuffing his face with those honey-glazed doughnuts he loved, his wispy-thin moustache twitching in frustration. Worse still, she sensed he was about to tell her something else she wasn't going to like.

Her stomach knotted, and the bitter taste of bile rose in the back of her throat. "Just say it. I know there's more."

Another sigh. More silence.

"Goddamn it, Antonio. It's my dad, right? You're coming for him?" Anger seethed in her, threatening to erupt. How could he do this to her? Pretend he was on her side, take her money, make promises! She was backed into a corner and, like it or not, had to swallow her anger... *for now.*

"Yup. But..."

"But what?" she was almost screaming now. She thought of her dad and how haggard he looked. The stress was sneaking up on him again. The investigation combined with the pressures of his job scared her. What if he had a heart attack or a nervous breakdown? Then what would become of her?

"Your parents have been asked to come down to the station. We need a set of prints from both of them."

Natalie puffed out a breath, then laughed so hard she nearly cried. Why on earth would they need her mother's prints? But something broke in her at that thought. It meant they were after either of her parents, and apparently it didn't matter which one. Lily was probably behind all of this. She'd gotten to Wilkins or Deluca and wriggled her way out of trouble yet again.

* * *

"What just happened?" Lily asked, stunned. They were still standing, and Aiden had just kissed her forehead.

Then he told her what Wilkins said, that they couldn't arrest her because, even though the ballistics report concluded the bullets came from her gun, the finger and palm prints weren't hers. They were back to circumstantial evidence. Since it was now clear she didn't fire the gun, there was even the possibility the weapon was planted.

She was confused. "Why didn't Wilkins tell me himself?"

"He said he called the diner first, then your cell and got no answer. Must be all the commotion in here. Can't hear a bloody thing! He figured I'd be with you, so he called me. Doesn't matter anyway, does it? It's good news no matter how it got to you." He smoothed her hair, and she thought he was going to kiss her again.

"Guess you're right," she said, and the relief that washed over her at the good news was too much to keep the smile from her lips.

"What happens next?"

He was still smiling. "You're gonna love this. Zander and Gabrielle Lyons are on their way to the station."

"No way!"

He nodded. "They need their prints."

"Both of them?"

"Yeah. Guess Wilkins finally had enough sense to listen to me. I had a chat with him earlier today and suggested he have a closer look at not just Zander but his wife. She had just as much motive to want your sister dead as Zander, maybe even more."

"I understand she'd be angry about the affair, but you'd think she'd be used to her husband's infidelities by now, and Sara had all kinds of money of her own. She didn't need Zander's to raise the baby." She shook her head. "It's hard for me to believe Gabrielle is capable of murder."

"You're not looking at it the right way. It wouldn't be because of money. It would be jealousy. Jealousy can make a person do all sorts of things. Don't underestimate the power of that emotion. Zander Lyons is a notorious philanderer, and if he had a love child with another woman, think of how it would make Gabrielle not only feel but also look to the others in the community. At any rate, we'll know more tomorrow. I'm gonna stop by to see Wilkins. Think I'll collect that paycheck after all."

Lily's eyes widened. "You weren't going to take your pay?"

He gave her a warm smile. "Not if they were going to arrest you."

So his job was just about done. As soon as they arrested Zander or Gabrielle, Aiden would no longer be needed. Should she ask what his plans were? What if he said he was going back to Chicago? She wasn't sure how she felt about that, but something very close to disappointment was creeping up on her.

"Can we get out of here now?" Aiden asked.

"To go where?"

"The cabin. Say you'll come."

She shook her head. "I want to go home. We can talk there if you like."

CHAPTER 23

"Rex!" Lily exclaimed as she pulled her Corolla into the driveway. He shouldn't be outside. When she'd left him that morning, she'd locked the house up tight and turned to catch the poor fellow looking forlornly at her through the front window.

She threw the car into park and jumped out. "Come here, boy." She bent to his level to coax him and he ran over, eager to greet his owner, wagging his tail and giving her a few sloppy kisses.

Aiden pulled into the driveway behind Lily and was quickly by her side, bending to pet the dog. "Something wrong?"

"I don't know how he got out." Lily stood and started toward the front door, holding Rex by the collar.

"Wait," Aiden called, stopping her with a hand on her wrist. "Take the dog and go sit in my truck."

He walked back with them and opened the door. Rex jumped in without hesitation, but Lily turned toward him, eyebrows arched. "Why?"

"Let me check around first. I'll be right back." He put a hand under her elbow and helped her into the passenger's seat, then popped open the glove compartment and took out his Magnum.

"Why do you need that?" Her voice rose with alarm.

He didn't answer her question. Instead, he seemed to change right in front of her. His eyes narrowed, his jaw tightened, and his lips thinned. "Lock the doors."

Aiden turned and walked slowly toward the house. He made his way up the front steps to the front door. It was locked. He checked the first-floor windows—all secure. Nothing looked broken or out of the ordinary, but when he walked around to the back, a door was wide open. He knew Lily was careful, that she was the type to lock the doors. He held the gun up and stepped through the doorway into the kitchen.

Every cupboard door had been thrown open, every drawer too, the contents pulled out or poured onto the floor.

He moved farther into the house. The furnishings were sparse, but what Lily did own was either ruined or damaged. The bookcases in the living room were overturned, and books lay strewn all over the room. Whoever did this had even picked up some of the novels and thrown them at the wall, hitting framed family photos and knocking them to the floor where they lay smashed.

The cozy-looking chair beside the bookcases had a kitchen knife stuck in the back of it.

Aiden stood still for a moment, listening for movement. Hearing nothing, he made his way upstairs. There were three bedrooms. One was an office, another a guest room, and then there was the master suite, Lily's bedroom. All had been vandalized. Once he'd checked every closet, room, and hiding place, he tucked his gun into the back of his waistband and fished out his cell phone.

Aiden left the house a few minutes later through the front door and made his way to the truck. He opened the passenger-side door where Lily sat with Rex on her knee.

"Someone did a job on your house. They broke in through the back. I guess so no one would be able to see what was happening from the road."

"Oh my God!" Lily moved Rex over to the driver's side and jumped out. She started toward the house. "How bad is it?"

Aiden jogged to her side. "Pretty bad. I called the sheriff's department. Someone's on the way. Probably shouldn't go in. They'll want to secure the scene."

"I just want to see." She opened the front door and stepped inside. A gasp escaped her and her hands flew to her mouth. "Who would do this?" She moved farther in, but Aiden stopped her with a gentle hand on the shoulder. "I don't understand." She began to cry and he pulled her into his arms.

"Shhh," he soothed, stroking her hair.

"What if I was home? I wouldn't have had any way to protect myself. I don't have my gun. What do you think they wanted? To hurt me?"

"Don't know." He let her go so she could have a look around. "Can you see if anything's missing from here? It may have been a robbery." He said the words but knew they were hollow. This was no robbery.

"I don't have anything worth stealing, really. I don't keep money in the house." She took a cursory glance around. "I can't tell."

She was flustered and had every right to be, but he needed her to come back to herself, to pay attention. "Your TV and laptop are still here. I saw them when I looked through the house. I don't know about jewelry though."

Lily shook her head. "I don't have any valuables." She sighed. "You don't think it was one of the Lyonses, or maybe they hired someone to do this?"

Aiden shook his head. "I doubt it. Why would they?"

They went back to the truck and waited for help. Minutes later, Deluca pulled into the long circular driveway and got out of his patrol car.

"You reported a break-in?" he said, looking from Aiden to Lily.

Aiden filled him in, and after taking statements, Deluca secured the scene, pulling shut the back door and wrapping yellow police tape around the porch. "Someone will be here shortly to dust for prints and collect any evidence, but you're going to have to find somewhere else to stay for a while. Deluca's gaze roamed up to Aiden's.

"Can she grab some stuff? You know, like personal items?" Aiden asked.

Deluca shook his head. "Sorry. You'll have to buy those things until we give you the all clear. Your insurance should pick up the tab. Just make sure to keep all your receipts."

"Can we go now?" Lily asked.

"Yes. We'll be in touch. I have your cell phone number."

"She'll be staying with me, deputy," Aiden said, and Lily didn't protest. She slipped her hand into his as they headed back to the truck.

As Aiden slid behind the wheel, he spied Deluca, cell phone in one hand and the other slamming the side of Lily's house with such force, Aiden could almost feel the anger in the blows, or was it frustration? God, he wished he could creep over and find out what was happening, but he had to go before Lily spotted him.

CHAPTER 24

They made a quick shopping trip before heading to the cabin, buying things Lily would need for her stay at Aiden's place—pajamas, toiletries, a couple of changes of clothes, dog food, and enough groceries so they wouldn't have to venture out unless they felt like it. Aiden splurged on crystal wineglasses. No more plastic cups.

"I'm glad you're here, but I wish it were under better circumstances," Aiden said while searching a drawer for a corkscrew. He'd placed a bottle of Cabernet on the counter in front of Lily along with the new glasses.

"None for me, thanks."

He stopped what he was doing and looked at her, shoulders deflated. "Really? I know it's kinda early, but I thought you could use a little something to help you relax."

She drew in a breath and held her thumb and pointer finger out an inch apart. "Very little."

Aiden carried their wine into the living room. Lily followed and took a seat on one of the couches. He sat beside her but gave her room.

"By the way, thank you. I don't know what I would have done if I'd gone into the house myself and found it…that way," Lily said.

He took her hand and she let him. "I'm glad I was there too. But it might be a good idea to invest in an alarm system."

Lily looked down at Rex sleeping by her feet. "Or a *real* guard dog." She laughed, sipped her wine, then leaned back into the softness of the couch. "I'm not going to let the break-in ruin things."

He tilted his head and looked at her. "Whadda ya mean?"

She took a long breath, then blew it out slowly. "I've never been one of those people who saw value in stuff, you know. Never wanted a big fancy house, never drove a status-symbol car—expensive jewelry is wasted on me. All I value is family." She barked a laugh. "Funny, isn't it? I've got a ton of money and no one to share it with." Then with a shrug of her shoulders, she continued, "But, like I said, I'm not going to be upset about what happened. It's only stuff, material things. It can all be replaced. I'm going to change gears and focus on the good. Life has been hell for months now. My sister murdered, me investigated. Finally, I'm in the clear and I haven't had time to let that sink in."

"You're one of those silver lining kinds of people, and I've always been a glass-half-empty guy myself."

She thought about that for a second. They were opposites. She believed in things unseen, an afterlife, fate, karma. Aiden, on the other hand, was pragmatic and practical, logical and analytical. Despite all he'd done to her, she realized he'd done it without really knowing her, and it was nice, *no*, more than just nice. It had been comforting and a huge relief to have him with her just now at her house, taking care of everything.

He inched over and tucked an errant strand of hair behind her ear. "Do you forgive me?"

She opened her mouth to speak, but shut it again and sighed. She wanted to forgive him, but was it wise? Would he hurt her again? And there was something else, if she was honest. She wanted to punish him, wanted him to work a bit before she said the words "I forgive you."

He leaned forward as if to reveal a secret. "I'm willing to try anything to win back your trust…and your heart, that is, if you'd ever given it to me." He pursed his lips and his brows knit together as he studied her.

Lily turned her gaze to the floor, not wanting him to see the truth in her eyes. She had given him her heart and, she knew, he still possessed it. "I opened up to you. Let myself be vulnerable and said things I'd never told anyone, and then I found out it was your *job* to pretend to like me. How do you think that makes me feel?" She wasn't angry, not really, not anymore, but she needed to know he understood how he'd made her feel.

He looked contrite. "From the moment we met, I saw something special in you. I had to keep reminding myself to stay professional, not fall for you. That's *never* happened to me before. True, when I first took the job, I thought there was a good chance you were guilty, but that was because Wilkins and Deluca had me convinced. Once I got to know you for myself, I…well, I hoped you were innocent because of how I felt about you, but it didn't take long before I *knew* you were."

He lifted her chin with a finger. "Do you forgive me?" he asked again, emotion coloring his words.

What was it about Aiden O'Rourke that melted her defenses? She did forgive him, but still, pride stood in her way. She sipped her wine, emptying the glass. "Maybe I will have a bit more."

Aiden went quickly to the kitchen, returned with the bottle, and filled her glass. She took a few more sips, wishing the Cabernet would hurry and work its magic. Maybe if the wine carried her away, she'd let her defenses down.

He was looking at her expectantly, and she was all too aware she hadn't answered his question. Why was she punishing herself as much as she was him?

"Do you believe in fate?" he asked.

"What?"

"Just answer my question."

She didn't hesitate. "You know I do."

"Well, I never did—not until I met you. Despite the circumstances that brought me here to Higgstown and to you, I believe we were meant to meet."

Could the universe really be so cruel? Taking people away from her only to replace them with someone else?

Why couldn't she have them all at the same time? "Even though we were brought together through tragedy?"

He nodded. "Kinda sucks but yeah. I think so."

Lily looked at Aiden and her heart set to beating triple time. Right in front of her was a chance at real happiness, at finding love, maybe even having a family again. The realization knocked the air from her lungs. In that moment she wanted to hug him, to cling to him and to say the words, but she couldn't.

CHAPTER 25

Natalie heard her parents enter the house from the garage. She watched as her dad walked past her to the bar in the great room and poured himself a Scotch. She'd gotten home just before them, quickly plucked up the Anne Rice novel sitting on the end table, and pretended to read. She thought her visit to Lily's house would release her pent-up rage, but it did nothing except set her more on edge.

Antonio had been calling and leaving messages. She knew she was going to catch hell for trashing Lily's place but really didn't give a shit. Now she eyed her father as he slammed back his drink and poured another.

Her mother clicked her way to the powder room around the corner, and Natalie heard a drawer slide open and then the familiar rattle of pills shaken from a bottle. Each went straight to their self-medication of choice. Things mustn't have gone well at the station.

"What happened, Daddy?" Natalie asked.

Zander settled beside her on the couch and gave her a smile, the kind that went all the way to his eyes, but there was something about the set of his jaw that let her know bad news was coming. "Nothing for you to worry your pretty little head about, honey. Just a stressful day, is all." He kissed her forehead, but she heard the wobble in his voice and saw he had the bloodshot eyes of a man with something on his mind. Even though he hadn't let the news slip from his lips, she felt it, like an annoying mosquito buzzing around her head.

"I don't believe you. Are you OK?"

Gabrielle came into the room. "I need a drink, too," she said to Zander.

He turned his attention from his daughter but first gave her a wink. "I heard you in the bathroom. What did you take? You can't have a drink if you took pills," he said to his wife.

"Never mind what I took. Pour me a goddamn drink and make it a double."

Zander got up and did as he was told, but held back on the double. He also watered it down, hoping she wouldn't notice.

She took the proffered drink with a smirk and sipped it. "Not very strong."

Natalie watched her mother. Her normally perfect coif was disheveled, and her hands trembled when she brought the glass to her lips.

"Can one of you please tell me what's going on?"

"Honey, maybe you should go and let me and your mother talk. Really, I don't want you to worry about a single thing," Zander said.

"Good Lord in heaven, my saint of a husband is trying to spare his daughter the bitter truth." Gabrielle dropped sloppily into an armchair, and Zander shot her a warning glare.

"Tell me!" Natalie yelled. "I'm not going anywhere until I know what's going on."

Gabrielle barked a laugh. "Well, you *should* know what's going on. You bloody well should, because it's all your fault." Her mother glared at her through narrowed, hate-filled eyes.

Natalie rubbed at her temples, which were beginning to pound. She needed a pill, something to calm the growing panic threatening to engulf her.

"That's enough out of you," Zander said sternly. "Go take more of your pills and get the hell out of here."

Gabrielle laughed. It was a chilling sound that filled Natalie with dread.

"She's going to know the truth even if they're the last words out of my mouth," Gabrielle said and leaned forward, eyeing her daughter. "A few days ago I found a gun under your bed, my darling girl. I picked it up, but put it back. Don't know why the hell you have it, but I figured you'd come around to telling me about it someday. Or, more likely, you'd tell your dad, since the two of you are like two peas in a pod. Anyway, turns out that gun is the murder weapon used to kill Sara Valier, and now it has my prints on it. You wanna tell me why *you* had that gun, or are you going to let me take the rap and go to jail?"

"I hid the gun," Zander said. He placed a hand on Natalie's shoulder and looked down at her. "Enough is enough. I'm going to the police to tell them it was me."

"Jesus, Zander. I picked it up. I held it my hand. My prints are on it, not yours." Gabrielle's words were beginning to slur. "They're not going to believe you. They want to wrap this up in a tidy little bow. They're coming after me!" She ran a hand over her face, smearing her glossy pink lipstick across a cheek as tears began to fall in black streaks down her face.

She's hideous, Natalie thought as she twisted away from her father and ran from the room. She could hear her parents' angry voices, arguing at full tilt. With palms slammed against her ears, she was an eight-year-old again, powerless over the turmoil in her life.

Grateful her parents hadn't come after her, she made her way to her father's office unseen, unlocked the top drawer of his desk, and grabbed the Beretta hidden there. She wasn't the only one in the family who snooped.

It was time to make this all go away.

CHAPTER 26

"So, I guess that's that then. You're not going to let me off the hook," Aiden said. He'd never been in a position like this before. Hopelessness washed over him. He was losing her. Hell, did he ever really have her in the first place?

"I...I do forgive you," Lily said finally.

His eyes widened and then he smiled as relief flooded him. Unfortunately, there was more to confess. If Lily was to forgive him fully, she had to know everything. Time to throw caution to the wind and lay all his cards on the table. No more lies. Lily meant too much to him.

This was a first. He didn't think of himself as a dishonest man, but because he was often surrounded by murderers and thieves and other not so nice people, deception came easily. Too easily. It had become his default after so many years. But Lily brought something out in him he hadn't felt in a long time, and that was the desire to be a good man, a man of integrity—not just a tough guy whose most dominant character trait was cynicism.

"I have something I need to tell you." His words were slow and deliberate.

Lily looked at him squinty-eyed, forehead furrowed. "Something *bad*?"

He looked away for an instant, gathered himself, then faced her again. "I hope you won't take it that way, but there are a few more things I need to tell you because I want you to forgive me for *everything*. I'm not going to keep anything from you, Lily."

She sat up straighter, her face a mask of fortitude. He could tell she was trying not to look upset. "I'm listening."

Aiden cleared his throat and began, "OK. Um, first things first, I'm ashamed to admit this, but I hired that thug who terrorized you at the diner just so I could rush in at the last minute and be a hero. You know, to get into your good graces so you'd trust me. But I swear to you, Lily, he never would have harmed a hair on your head. I told him to make sure you didn't get hurt."

Anger curled her fingers into fists. "OK." Her tone was icy.

He could see the wheels turning. She was weighing things in her mind. "What are you thinking?"

She huffed and shook her head. "That I threw a pot of scalding coffee in this guy's face and cracked the umbrella stand across the back of his neck. Probably really hurt him." She sighed. "But then again, any man willing to take a job that involves terrifying a woman deserves what he got."

Aiden laughed with relief. He noticed her shoulders fall and her hands unclench. He was afraid she was going to tell him to take her to back to town, that she'd sleep in her office at the diner.

"I'm sorry, Lily. God, I'm such an ass. Being a private investigator has made me cynical and untrusting of everyone. But it's all I've ever known, all I know how to do."

He leaned close to kiss her, but she turned away. He wasn't off the hook just yet.

"Was *everything* you told me the last time I was here, the night we…was it *all* lies?"

"Most of it was true. Everything I said about my parents was true. What wasn't true was that I was ever in love, ever engaged. I didn't want to get married, that is until I met you, but right now, you probably hate my guts." He paused and turned her face to him with a finger. "I'm falling in love with you."

Despite her apparent anger, a smile found its way to her lips, but she remained silent.

"Don't leave me hanging. I've never said those words to anyone before." The fire of embarrassment crept up from his collar until he could feel his cheeks burning. The power had shifted, and the ball was clearly in her court.

Finally, she spoke. "I don't think I could take another heartbreak."

He slid over to her and pulled her into his arms. "I won't ever hurt you again." Aiden entwined a hand in her hair and pressed her close to him with the other. This time she let him kiss her.

Why couldn't she say those three little words? He'd opened up to her and let himself be vulnerable, but she just couldn't let her guard down completely. She saw the disappointment in his eyes and that he pretended to be fine. She pretended too.

But their time together was not without its merits. Now, with nothing hanging over their heads, no hidden agenda, they chatted. It was as if she was getting to know him for the first time all over again, but this time it was the real Aiden. The hours passed like minutes.

She even let her guard down enough to be happy for just a while. More than anything, she wanted to look forward to the future and to better times. Despite their conversation, and the fact it calmed her, even made her hopeful, Aiden's confession and her sister's murder still weighed heavy on her heart. Would she ever be rid of the black cloud of despair that followed her, nagged her, churned her belly with anxiety? Would she ever feel safe again?

"Are you sure it was one of the Lyonses who killed my sister?" Lily asked.

Aiden took in a deep breath and nodded. "I'd lay money on it. Something Zander said set off alarm bells. He told me Sara wanted an abortion as much as he did, that they were in agreement over it. That stood out because of what you told me. That she wanted the baby. I'm betting Wilkins arrests one of them soon."

She wanted an end to the accusations as well as justice for her sister, but hearing that Zander lied about Sara wanting an abortion pushed her buttons to the max. There was so much going on inside her, so many emotions— anger, frustration, relief, even joy. She couldn't help but feel selfish though. She'd gained from Sara's death in every possible way, inheriting her money and meeting Aiden. Why did it feel so wrong to feel good?

She should be over the moon, jumping up and down with excitement. Hadn't this been what was missing in her life? Someone to love? She needed to push the destructive emotions away. Stuff them into a dark corner of her mind where she could deal with them later.

"I know talking about your sister depresses you." Aiden stroked Lily's cheek. "But there's more going in that head of yours, isn't there?"

Hot tears filled her eyes. "I don't deserve to be happy. I don't deserve all that money in my bank account, and I don't deserve you either, Aiden."

"Sometimes good things come from bad circumstances."

She wasn't sure she really believed that. Suddenly, it was as if the walls were closing in. She needed fresh air. "You wanna get out of here? We can take Rex."

Aiden smiled. "Absolutely."

* * *

Holy Cross Cemetery was large for a town the size of Higgstown and confusing for those who didn't know exactly where they were headed. But Lily knew the way, and took Aiden and Rex directly to the grave site she was seeking.

The oldest part of the cemetery was dotted with headstones, some so dilapidated they'd toppled over. In the newer section, flat brass plaques were used with the name of the deceased and two important dates stamped onto the surface.

Lily handed Rex's leash to Aiden, who took it readily. Crouched down now, she wiped clean two plaques with a Kleenex from her pocket. "This is Mom on the left and Sara on the right," she said.

Lily kissed her palm and laid it flat on one of the plaques. "Sara, I miss you every day. I love you with all my heart and I'm sick over what happened to you, but I need your blessing before I can go on and live a life with Aiden." Tears flowed and she blotted them away with the back of her hand. "So, if you could, would you please give me some kind of sign that you approve?"

Then she turned her attention to her mother's grave. "Mom, I miss you, too. I'm lonely without you and Sara, and sometimes I get jealous knowing you two are together and I'm stuck here trying to find a reason to live. But I've met someone." She smiled and looked up at Aiden. "Just wanted to let you know what's going on, Mom. I love you and next time, I'll bring you roses and some tulips for Sara." She blew each of them a kiss.

Aiden held out a hand to help her to her feet. "You think I'm foolish for thinking they can hear me, don't you?" she said.

"No. Not if it makes you feel better."

Lily cupped his face in her hand. "I'll make a believer out of you yet."

"I know you'll give it your best shot." He smiled. "What now? Wanna grab a cup of coffee or something?"

She shook her head. "No. We've got another stop to make."

* * *

It's the dead center of town, but everyone's dying to get in. That stupid line her dad always said when they drove past the cemetery ran through Natalie's head now as she sat cross-legged under an enormous weeping willow watching Aiden and Lily. The yellowed leaves were beginning to fall, but there were still enough clinging to the large overhanging branches to provide cover. A lot of the snow had melted and the clearing under the tree was free of it, but the earth beneath her was cold and damp, sending a chill up her spine and making her wish she had a blanket to sit on. Her jacket, though warm, was too short to tuck under her butt to help fight the chill.

Every so often, she caressed the cold metal of her father's Beretta, which weighed heavily in her jacket pocket. This weapon was different from that toy Lily called a gun, with its stupid pearl handle made pretty for a woman.

Power surged through her knowing the gun was close. With it she could make anyone do anything.

CHAPTER 27

"It's not your usual day for a visit," came Gail's cheery voice from behind the reception desk.

"Sorry, Gail. I know. Should I have called?" Lily replied.

In all the time she'd been visiting with the residents of the center, Lily never strayed from her schedule aside from the times she stopped by to pick up Mrs. G. But none of the other residents knew of those visits. She'd phone ahead and Gail always had Mrs. G. ready and waiting for her in the foyer. Lily didn't want the others to be angry or envious of her friend, but today was different. It was important to her that the only people who never judged her got to meet Aiden. She'd get an honest assessment out of her friends at the center and was especially looking forward to what Mrs. G. had to say.

"No, this is a wonderful surprise. Everyone will be happy to see you." Gail moved from her perch behind the desk and came around to stand beside Lily. Placing a slender hand on Lily's arm, she raised a brow. "Now, tell me. Who is this handsome stranger you've brought with you today? And I don't mean Rex." She bent and patted the dog, who offered a few slobbery kisses. Whenever Lily brought Rex with her on visits, he charmed the residents and staff by being his laid-back old self, always ready with a kiss.

Lily smiled. "This is Aiden."

Aiden shook Gail's hand. "I've heard a lot about you. On the way over, Lily told me all about this place and the wonderful people here." He smiled, showing off his dimple.

Gail fanned herself, feigning embarrassment. "Why, thank you, Miss Valier." She turned to Lily. "I appreciate all your kind words, but I have to ask, where have you been hiding this gorgeous man of yours?"

It was Lily's turn to be embarrassed. How could she answer Gail's question? How absurd was it that she'd fallen for Aiden so quickly?

Before she could answer, Aiden spoke. "We've only been dating a little while." He took Rex's leash and wrapped an arm around Lily's shoulder.

Silently, Lily thanked him for saving her. She'd known Gail for a long time and had never mentioned a man in her life.

Lily and Aiden hung their coats in the small closet by the door and brushed their shoes clean on the institutional-looking mat in the entranceway. Lily felt guilty about not having her usual stash of puzzles, magazines, DVDs, and books. "No gifts this time but I think everyone will love visiting with Rex. I haven't brought him in since summer."

Gail waved a hand. "All anyone here wants is to visit with you, Miss Lily. You know how much the residents love you." Suddenly, Gail's demeanor changed. Her smile disappeared and worry lined her face. "Before you go in though, I have to tell you something." Her eyes darted away from Lily, then back, her lips pressing into a grim line. "Mrs. G. fell ill a few days ago. I was going to call, but thought it better to wait a while before alarming you. In case she got better."

Lily's blood drained to her feet. "Is she OK? What happened?"

"Darling, I know what she means to you, but you've been coming around here long enough to know how things always end in this place. It's a sad reality, but one we've all got to face someday. Now, why don't you and your handsome young man go and have your visit. No one but God knows which way the tide will turn for Mrs. G. You can visit with her in her room if you like." She gave a halfhearted, sympathetic smile.

Lily knew she was right, but couldn't help be upset no one had called. Mrs. G. was like a grandmother to her.

"Thanks, Gail," she said stiffly, before heading down the hallway into the brightly lit common room.

"Lily? My, my, what a nice surprise," said Irene Scott as the ninety-two-year-old slowly made her way over. Her words alerted the others, who turned their heads one by one like meerkats on the Kalahari to spot Lily, Aiden, and Rex making their way into the room.

The TV was loud and the lights so bright that Aiden looked dizzy. He seemed to get a kick out of how all the residents were drawn to Lily like a moth to a flame.

"So, Lily tells us you and her are dating?" A man in a fedora and sports coat said. He sat down beside Aiden, rickety knees cracking and popping, then stared at him with no apparent regard for social conventions.

"Leave the man alone," an elderly lady in a red jacket said as she lowered herself to the couch on the other side of Aiden. She placed a gnarled hand on his knee and looked up at him, studying his face.

Lily's eyes lit up at Aiden's squirming discomfort.

"So, are you, honey? Dating, I mean," the old woman asked, picking up the thread of the conversation and running with it.

He eyed Lily for help. "Um, yeah. Lily and I are dating."

"Whadda ya do for a living? You got a good job? You can take care of our Lily?" the man asked.

Lily finally broke in. "Mr. Piccione." She smiled. "I can take care of myself."

"Uh-uh, no way. If this guy has intentions toward ya, he's gotta be a good provider. He's gotta take care of you." He turned back to Aiden. "Just what are your intentions? And what kinda name is Aiden anyway? Never heard it before. All these silly new names they have these days." He shook his head.

Lily laughed and made introductions. "The man giving you the third degree is Mr. Piccione, the lovely lady to your left is Irene Scott…" She continued, pointing and naming names until each and every one of the residents had been introduced to Aiden.

A sudden frown appeared on Lily's face. "Anyone know how Mrs. G is doing? Gail told me she's sick."

Irene pouted and sighed. "Not so well, I'm afraid, dear. She's in her room. Had to take the oxygen today." The old woman tapped her chest. "Think it's her heart."

Lily's own heart sped up at her words. "Would it be OK if I leave Rex here with you?" Lily asked Mr. Piccione. "I want to go see Mrs. G."

"Sure. Gimme that leash. But when you get back, I want answers from your fella." He winked.

With a heavy heart, Lily forced a smile and waved at her friends as she made her way to Mrs. G.'s room. Before she even entered, she could hear the soft in and out of her friend's respiration. Aiden stayed in the entranceway as she crept farther into the semidarkness. Finally, she made out the woman's tiny figure. Hair, shoe-polish black, fanned out around her tiny, pale face, making it look as if she was lying on a dark pillowcase.

Lily snapped on the lamp beside her. An oxygen tube hugged the woman's nostrils, and an IV needle had been inserted and taped to the back of her papery-skinned hand. A machine kept the beat of her heart, which was slow but steady.

Bouquets of flowers in vases, plants, and get-well cards sat on the windowsill. A lump formed in Lily's throat. Was she going to lose her friend soon? Mrs. G. had lived in the Evelyn Harrison Seniors Center for decades, and Lily couldn't imagine the place without her. A tiny dynamo, her friend was always moving and doing and taking care of everyone.

Tears stung Lily's eyes. She blinked, letting them slide down her cheeks, but dabbed them away before pulling up a chair to sit beside her friend, not wanting her to see her distress if she woke. With loving gentleness, she took Mrs. G.'s hand and sat with her while she slept. She glanced back at Aiden, who was still standing in the shadows, leaning against the metal door frame, arms folded. He nodded, letting her know he was fine. Lily gestured him in, but he waved her off and mouthed, *Later*.

Then the weight of another hand landed on hers and Lily saw that Mrs. G. had clamped the hand free of the IV over her own. Her eyes were open and she was smiling.

Lily smiled back, then bent to kiss a blue-veined hand. "How are you feeling?"

"Like the old woman I am." Her voice was raspy but surprisingly strong. "It's nice to see you, angel."

Mrs. G. always called her that. Not honey or sweetheart or dear but angel. There was love in that word for Lily.

"Is there anything I can do for you? Anything you need?"

"Oh, no. Look around here. I've had visitors. Plenty of people, all wanting to do something for me." Her eyes began to cloud with tears. "I know the truth, angel. They're coming to say their good-byes."

"Don't say that. You're going to feel better soon." Her words felt hollow and she feared Mrs. G. wasn't buoyed by them.

"Everybody's got an expiration date and mine is coming on fast. Don't let my silly old tears fool you. I'm ready to go when the Lord calls me home. It's just that…" The old woman stumbled, looking off in the distance, seemingly searching for the right words before she continued, "I don't like good-byes. I'm gonna miss everyone." More tears blossomed in the corners of her eyes, and Lily grabbed a Kleenex from the night table to dab them away.

Mrs. G. had hold of Lily's heartstrings and was yanking hard. How could she reply? Nothing she could say would make things better. Good-byes were horrible. She'd had more than her share, but she did have faith there was a place beyond here. She didn't know if heaven was the right word, but another *dimension* perhaps—where her sister and mother now lived. Souls are connected forever; love never died. She *hoped* that was true anyway, and that's what she told Mrs. G.

The old woman's eyes brightened. "I think you're right, angel. The people on the other side told me the same thing."

Lily's brow furrowed. "People? What people? And on the other side of what?" This she hadn't expected, and she wondered briefly about her friend's mental state.

But wisdom shone in Mrs. G.'s eyes. "I think you already know. You forget what you just told me already?" She gave a little laugh. "The veil thins when you're as old as I am and when you're on the brink of death." She patted Lily's hand. "Ah, angel, don't you worry. I'm not losing my mind, but I've *seen* the people on the other side. You know, the place where we go when we die. That's how I know my time is coming. Think they're checking in and want me to know they'll be there for me when I pass over."

Lily was intrigued now and surprised at the wisdom in Mrs. G.'s words. "Who are these people?"

"Loved ones, friends and family who've gone before me. Saw my parents and my husband. Only thing is I can't get to them. And they can't get all the way here to me. I see their lips moving but can only hear them speaking in my head." Mrs. G's hands tightened on Lily's. "It comforts me so much."

Was what she was saying true or just the imaginings of an old woman on the brink of death? Lily held the same beliefs, but she and Mrs. G. hadn't spoken about these things before. Either way, she figured it didn't matter, just as long as her friend was finding comfort in her faith.

The old woman shifted, trying to push herself to a sitting position, but Lily laid a hand on her shoulder. "I'll help you. Just stay there." She pushed a button and a mechanical clang set the bed in motion. Lily stopped once it was at a slight incline. "Better?"

"Much." She sighed then raised a finger in the air. "Oh, before I forget, go over there." She pointed to a vase of flowers on the window ledge. "You're supposed to look right in the middle."

Lily laughed. What could possibly be in the middle of a flower arrangement that would be meaningful to her? "Are you serious?"

"Oh yes, Sara wants you to."

Gooseflesh pricked her arms. "Sara who?" Her words were slow and cautious. She dare not think of the only Sara she knew.

"Your sister of course," Mrs. G. answered with a spark of mischief in her eyes.

Lily's hand flew to her chest in an effort to calm her banging heart. No, this couldn't be happening. She was making it up.

Slowly, Lily rose, and on legs that felt as if they were made of straw, she walked over to the vase sitting on the ledge. It was jammed with flowers of every sort and color. With shaking hands, she parted them and peered down. In the center, cut shorter than the others, was a pink tulip.

She plucked it out and stared unbelieving. Tulips were Sara's favorite flower.

"You gonna tell me what it means?" Mrs. G. asked eagerly.

Lily thought for a second, then turned to Aiden and waved him in. This time he came. "Mrs. G., this is Aiden.

He's very important to me, and I want you to meet him. I think the tulip was Sara's way of telling me I should go on with my life and be happy. It's been hard losing my sister, and I felt like I didn't have a right to my own happiness because her life ended so tragically. She's giving me permission." Lily grinned up at Aiden. In turn, his face crinkled into a smile.

Aiden turned to Mrs. G. "It's a pleasure to meet you."

She smiled at him for a moment, taking him in, studying his face. "What a handsome fellow," Mrs. G. finally said to Lily. "You two gonna get married?"

They shared a laugh at the directness of the questions they'd been facing from the residents. Reaching a certain age had its privileges, and one of them seemingly was a complete and utter lack of boundaries.

"Who knows what the future holds." Aiden winked.

CHAPTER 28

In their absence, the cabin had grown cold. Aiden went directly to the fireplace and began to build the perfect blaze, a task he'd grow adept at.

"What did you think of Mrs. G.?" Lily stood behind him, watching as he stoked the flames.

"She's lovely."

"That's it?"

"I'm sorry about what she's going through. It must be hard getting old and knowing you only have a limited time left on earth."

Lily took his hand and led him to the couch. "But she's at peace with the idea of passing. You heard her."

Aiden laughed. "I'm not sure we're on the same page when it comes to that sort of thing."

"What do you mean by, 'that sort of thing'?"

"You know, all that living in another dimension when we die mumbo jumbo. I think when our time's up, we just cease to exist. Turn to dust and that's it."

Aiden had told her a few times what his thoughts were on the subject, but it was such a big part of her world view and faith that the differences in their philosophies bothered her.

"Do we have to talk about his now?" He nibbled at her neck, planting feathery kisses up and down her throat, finally ending with a lingering kiss at the hollow of her neck.

Heat bloomed in her cheeks as the flush of excitement ran through her. Why did her body have to betray her?

He took her hand and kissed it, then scooped her up into his arms and made his way to the loft. She let him, powerless, as if he'd cast a spell.

* * *

Natalie's cell phone rang just as she entered the house. She'd had a long day of following Aiden and Lily around to stupid places like cemeteries and old folks' homes. Were they fixated on death or something? Or was it because Halloween was just days away that their inner morbid was surfacing?

Not in the mood to chat with anyone, she glanced at her phone, ready to hit "ignore," but it was Antonio's name on the screen again.

"What is it?" she said, putting up a brave front, but fearing his response. She'd been living off coffee, doughnuts, and her mother's stupid cupcakes for days now. Her hand shook so badly she could barely keep the phone against her ear.

Antonio sighed. "You sitting down?"

Natalie was in the powder room now, sorting through the various bottles of pills her mother kept there. Finally, she found the one she wanted, popped the top, and swallowed a tiny pink pill. The knot of worry unraveling like a snake in her belly would soon calm. She put down the lid of the toilet seat and sat, preparing herself for bad news. "Sitting now."

"OK, I'm not going to beat around the bush. Wilkins is on his way to your house. Your mother's about to be arrested."

She wasn't surprised; she knew her mother's prints were on that gun, but yesterday she'd been too angry to give a shit. Hell, she would have opened the front door for Sheriff Wilkins herself. Now though, fear gripped her in hard, unyielding hands, and she nearly dropped the phone. They were coming for her mother.

Why did she care now? Because now it was *real*, and as much as she didn't like to admit it, even though she hated her mother and sometimes even wished her dead, she didn't *really* want her to go to jail. What would become of her if her family was torn apart? She was grown but just barely. She still needed them.

Natalie eyed the pill bottle and contemplated taking another, or maybe a handful. Instead, she pocketed it for later.

"Her finger and palm prints were a match to the murder weapon; she had motive and no alibi," Antonio continued. "I'm sorry. I know how hard you tried to keep

Wilkins off your dad's scent but…" He hesitated. "Maybe she did it, Natalie. Isn't it better it's your mom and not your dad? I know how close you are to him and—"

"Fuck off. You're a piece-of-shit cop. All you did was take my money and for what? You didn't keep me safe." She melted to the floor, dropping the phone and banging her head on the marble. The pain pierced through her forehead into her temples, but she needed it; she wanted it. She had to feel something other than her own heart breaking.

Antonio's voice echoed from her phone. She plucked it up and smashed it down on the floor. One loud crack and it shattered, rendered useless. She picked up the pieces and threw them into the waste-paper basket.

She could hear her parents' muffled voices somewhere nearby. Where were they? In the library? In the great room? They hadn't come running. That meant they hadn't heard her tantrum. Should she warn them? No, it was too late for that.

There was only one thing left to do.

CHAPTER 29

Natalie made her way to her father's bar and nosed around until she found what she was looking for. Everclear, one of the highest proof liquors ever made. She knew it was there, had seen it, even tried it once. After knocking back a shot, which she'd even watered down, it felt as if she'd been stabbed in the throat. The liquor was actually flammable and even had a label on it warning against drinking it straight. Horrible stuff but it was just what she needed. She took four bottles from the well-stocked bar and stuffed them in her leather satchel.

Then she went in search of more supplies and her backup phone. The SIM card from the smashed cell was salvageable, and she slid it into the older model. She'd charge the battery in the car.

Natalie parked at the bottom of Aiden's driveway, pulling off to the side as close to the pines as she could get without slipping into the ditch. She was sure her parents hadn't heard her leave. Let them worry, if they even realized she was gone. They didn't care about her anyway. Why should she care about them? Proper parents, good parents, took care of their kids. They didn't cheat. They didn't drink themselves into oblivion or take pills. They didn't throw the word "divorce" around, scaring the shit out of their kid.

Fueled by self-righteousness and self-pity, Natalie exited the SUV, threw her satchel over her shoulder, and yanked on a knitted hat, ready for her last-ditch effort to make everything safe in her world again. She had two plans, though the sinking feeling that Plan A more than likely wouldn't pan out saddened her. The thought of implementing Plan B calmed her despite what it entailed.

Plunging her hands deep into the pockets of her down-filled jacket, she caressed the frigid metal of the Beretta's grip. Gently, she placed a finger on the trigger. She wouldn't apply pressure, not yet, but her heartbeat slowed just having it in her hand. Power was what the gun gave her, the power to persuade. The power to take life. She knew how people saw her—they couldn't imagine she was capable of killing anyone. After all, wasn't she just a troubled teenager?

The night was wintry despite the fact it was technically still autumn, and it was dark, the only light coming from the stars and crescent moon. It'd be awesome to take the time to appreciate the night sky. If only she didn't have so many worries and so many loose ends that needed tying. The pill she'd downed earlier was at the height of its effect, calming her and bolstering her determination.

Trudging up the hill toward the cabin, her boot-clad feet crunched in what was left of the snow. Her thighs ached and burned as she made her way up the incline until finally, she was at the front door of the cabin. Breathing heavily, she crept onto the porch and peered through a sidelight. No lights on, but Lily's and Aiden's vehicles were in the driveway. They were home. Probably in bed. She shook her head in disgust. The Valier sisters were quick to hop into a man's bed.

Damn, how much easier it would have been if Lily had gone to her own home, alone. But she'd been to blame for that. She'd forced Lily out of her house and into Aiden's cabin by breaking in and trashing the place. Stupid move, yes, but what was done was done. It would have been easier to do what she came to do without a man around, especially one the size of Aiden O'Rourke, but she reminded herself that a gun was a great equalizer and she wasn't afraid to use it if she had to.

She tried the door handle. It clicked open.

Lily awoke with a start and sat up, her heartbeat like a sprinter's. It took a moment to gather her bearings, but once she realized she was with Aiden, in Aiden's cabin, in Aiden's bed, she calmed.

Moments of terror charging at her like a stalker in the night had been plentiful at home in her own bed, the fear clawing its way to the surface of her mind so forcefully at times, it stole her breath. Things were different now.

Lily looked over at a gently snoring Aiden. It was not an annoying snore, but a cute and comforting sound that made her feel safe.

She heard Rex walking around downstairs. They'd made a bed for him in front of the fireplace so he'd be comfortable and warm for the night. It wasn't just the click of his nails that carried up to the open loft but a low growl too.

Was Rex really growling? He was usually so quiet, never even barked when someone came to the door. Lily cocked her head, listening hard.

It came again, this time louder, followed by a bark.

She jumped out of bed, quickly dressed and contemplated waking Aiden but thought better of it. Maybe being in a strange house made Rex uneasy. After all, he'd never slept anywhere but at home. She peered over at Aiden, who'd stirred but hadn't woken. Must be nice to sleep so soundly, the sign of an unburdened mind.

Lily padded down the stairs, the only light coming from the embers still burning in the fireplace. Once at the bottom, she ran a hand along the wall, feeling for a light switch, but wasn't familiar enough with the layout of the cabin to find one.

"Don't move," came a furious whisper.

An icy-fingered tendril of dread traced its way down her spine, and a small sound came and died in her throat. Someone was crouched by the front door.

"Not much of a watchdog you've got, Lily." A woman. It was a woman! Her fear fell a notch until the figure stood, and Lily caught sight of the glint of metal in her hand.

Her breath caught in her throat and she stepped backward. "Who are you? What did you do to Rex?"

A laugh. "Your stupid dog's outside. Don't you people lock your doors? All I had to do was open it, and your mangy mutt came out to greet me."

Concern for Rex momentarily overrode her fear, and Lily peered past the woman through the sidelight in an effort to spot her dog. Then came the familiar scratching of a paw against wood, Rex's way of asking to be let back in. He'd be cold, but at least he was alive. Relief washed through her.

From what Lily could make out, the woman was tall, and despite the puff of her unzipped winter jacket, she looked scrawny.

"Who are you?"

"Keep your voice down. I know that PI is upstairs. You don't want me to have to shoot him, do you?"

Lily's heart leaped into her throat. This time when she spoke, it was a whisper. "Please, just tell me what you want."

The woman stepped toward Lily and stuck the gun in her ribs. "Move," she growled, pushing her toward the living room. A knitted hat was pulled down low on the woman's forehead, making it difficult for Lily to get a good look at her face. Did she know her? There was something familiar in that voice.

"Sit," the woman commanded once they were by the couches.

When she sat, the stranger stood in front of her. The burning logs in the fireplace threw more than enough light for Lily to finally see the woman's face. She was just a girl, not a woman. "Natalie?"

"Shut up."

The Natalie Lyons that Lily knew was needy and lonely, certainly nothing like this crazy-eyed girl in front of her now.

"Sara destroyed my life," Natalie began. "Your slut of a sister gets herself pregnant and ruins my parents' marriage, then the stupid bitch gets shot and everyone thinks my dad did it."

A flush of anger burned in Lily's chest and crawled its way up her neck to her cheeks. "Don't you think your dad had a little something to do with my sister getting pregnant? And maybe even with her murder?"

Pain speared Lily as the butt of the gun crashed into her jaw, sending her sprawling across the couch. A scream started to form in her throat, but for Aiden's sake, she let it die there.

"Shut up, bitch. Your sister was nothing but the town slut. My *mother's* going to prison because of her."

Lily worked her jaw, not sure if it was broken. A knife-like jab tore into her temples when she opened her mouth. Slowly, she pushed her way back to sitting. "What did you say?" Each word sent another stab of pain through her head.

"My mother is being blamed for your sister's murder. She's probably been arrested already."

Lily's suspicions had leaned toward Zander, but as she and Aiden had discussed earlier, Gabrielle had a damn good reason to want Sara dead too. "Then justice is served."

Natalie sat on the coffee table in front of her, their knees so close they were touching. "No, it hasn't been and do you know why?" She didn't wait for an answer. "Because my mother didn't kill your sister. I did." She spoke slowly and with purpose, words meant to shock.

Lily was struck again—the blow this time to her heart.

"But you're going to take the blame. You're going to confess." Natalie jabbed a finger at Lily's chest.

Fury pushed Lily to her feet, hands fisted by her sides. She swung at the girl and missed. Natalie, younger and faster, moved quickly out of the way, turning and twisting to her left. Now she had the gun jabbed into the small of Lily's back.

"You're coming with me, and we're going to see Deputy Deluca. You'll confess or I'll kill you and the man you just slept with."

Lily straightened and planted her feet defiantly, rooting to the spot. "I'm not going anywhere. You need me alive. How can I confess if I'm dead?"

She heard the girl's labored breaths and sighs of exasperation. With the barrel of the gun pushed uncomfortably into the hollow of Lily's back, Natalie grabbed her phone and punched in a number. "I'm at Aiden's cabin. Get over here now."

"Who'd you call?" Lily asked, trying to inch away.

"Stop. Don't take another step."

Lily kept moving. Slowly, slowly, she moved away from Natalie. Once she was a safe distance away, she turned to face the girl. The gun was no longer aimed at her but at Aiden, who stood stock-still halfway down the stairs.

"Time for Plan B," Natalie whispered.

CHAPTER 30

Aiden's heart beat steady and strong, his instincts on high alert as he crept slowly down the stairs. In the dim light he could make out Lily and another woman. Both had their backs to him as he carefully moved forward and that was good. He cursed himself for not locking the front door, and although he didn't know what was happening yet, his gut told him it was nothing good.

He'd only had time to pull on jeans, and although shirtless and sockless, pinpricks of sweat erupted all over his body in the cool air.

He wondered where Rex was. Why hadn't the dog protected Lily? Where was he now? Aiden's heart sank at the prospect of his demise.

The stairs creaked beneath his weight, stilling him. Something else stopped him too. The woman faced him, and a glint of metal flashed, revealing itself as a gun pointed at his chest.

"Sit," she said, but it was Lily she was talking to. "You move; I shoot him."

"What do you want?" Aiden called.

The woman walked slowly backward and reached out with a hand, feeling for the light switch. Finding it, she flicked it on. Her eyes darted between Aiden and Lily, keeping the gun trained on the more dangerous of the two, Aiden.

"Come down here and sit on the other couch."

He held his hands up where she could see them, walked the rest of the way down the stairs, and did as he was told.

"Hey! I know you. Natalie Lyons, right?" He tried to sound as harmless as possible, even friendly as he took a seat. He threw Lily a look, sending a message everything would be OK. After all, he could handle Natalie. She was just a scrawny, young girl.

"Why are you here, Natalie? I'm sure whatever's bothering you can be discussed civilly. You don't need that gun." He waved a dismissive hand. "Why don't you put it down and we'll talk."

Natalie's lips turned up in a snarl. "I'm not just some troubled kid who needs a hug to make everything better."

Aiden noticed her finger tightening on the trigger. He had to say something to calm her and fast. "Look, we all know you don't intend to use that thing. Please, Natalie, put it down before you accidentally hurt someone." He smiled warmly and patted the spot beside him. "Come sit, and Lily and I will help you."

She steadied her arm by grasping her wrist. "I have no use for you."

"This is ridiculous," he tried again.

She pulled the trigger. Two shots rang out. One caught Aiden in the shoulder, the other bored into the flesh of his abdomen, sending him flailing backward. Surprise registered momentarily before his face shriveled in a look of pain. This couldn't be happening.

"No!" Lily screamed and ran to him.

Natalie didn't bother to pull her away, only opened her pill bottle and downed three more. She'd just shot a man. So what? It really didn't feel as if she'd done something wrong. It was the right thing to do under the circumstances. He was dangerous and might have jumped up and grabbed the gun off her at any moment. After all, he'd been trained for such things. She smiled inwardly. She'd just outwitted him, and it felt damn good.

He'd underestimated her. People did that all the time, and she was sick of it. Always trying to placate her. Mother plying her with those stupid cupcakes; Dad, hugging her and calling her honey, taking her to doctor after doctor as if something was wrong with her. She shrugged off her satchel and set it on the floor, opening it.

"How does it feel to be alone again?" she said to Lily. "Alone, just like I am?"

Lily was too preoccupied to answer. With blood-slicked hands, she tried to staunch the flow bubbling from Aiden's abdomen. She grabbed the blanket from the back of the couch and pressed it onto the wound in his gut. His shoulder was a mess too, but Lily kept her hands rooted to the worst of the wounds.

"Won't do you any good. He's as good as dead." Natalie's words were punctuated by a sigh of contentment.

Headlights lit the room, and a moment later, the door flew open. Deputy Antonio Deluca ran in with Rex behind him. The dog sauntered over to his bed by the fire, turned in a circle, and curled up.

"Thank God!" Lily yelled. "Call an ambulance. Call the sheriff. She just shot Aiden!"

"Holy shit, Natalie. What the hell?" Antonio bellowed, taking in the scene.

Natalie smiled, her eyes heavy-lidded. "I shot the private dick and now I'm watching him die." Her words were flat as if she were reading off a menu.

Antonio's hand flew to the butt of his revolver.

"Draw that gun and you die too," Natalie said. The drugs may have dulled her senses but not enough to make her careless. She noticed Deluca was out of uniform. He had no cuffs, no radio, no Mace.

"I don't understand why you want to hurt these innocent people. If you put the gun down now, I might be able to help you. But if Aiden dies, you'll go to prison for the rest of your life." He moved to grab his cell. "I have to call an ambulance."

A bullet sent him skittering backward. He crashed to the hardwood, the back of his skull no longer there, splattered instead on the wall behind him.

CHAPTER 31

A nightmare was unfolding in front of Lily. Deputy Deluca was dead. There was no doubt about it. Blood and brain matter speckled the pale pine wall beside the fireplace, absurdly bringing to mind an abstract painting she'd once seen in a museum, a Jackson Pollock. Nothing seemed real. She felt nothing, not even fear. Time seemed to have slowed, and the only thing Lily was aware of was the whoosh of blood pulsing in her ears.

With effort, she pulled her attention from Deluca and Natalie. She had to think about Aiden now. Had to focus, gather her wits. Was he still breathing? She felt for a pulse and found one, slow and weak, but it was there! She wanted to cry with relief.

Natalie was standing by the fireplace, staring at her, *grinning* at her. Eyes half closed, watching and waiting for Aiden to die.

"What do you want me to do, Natalie? I'll do whatever you say. I'll confess to murdering Sara if you want. I'll say

Aiden came at you and you protected yourself. That you shot him in self-defense, just please call an ambulance!"

Natalie bent to her haunches, letting the gun dangle playfully from a finger. "He's taking too long to bleed out, maybe he needs another bullet. To the head this time?" She seemed not to be addressing Lily, but to be giving voice to her thoughts. She raised the gun and Lily scrambled to cover Aiden with her own body. It would do no good, she knew. The bullet would just kill them both, but it was all she could think to do.

"Nah, I'll let him die slowly." She lowered the weapon. "Better that way." Her expression was one of deep contentment, as if she'd never been happier in all her life.

Lily tried again. "I promise I won't go back on my word. I'm sorry for all the things that happened to your family, but if you don't act fast, your mother will be arrested. She'll be sent to the maximum-security prison in Bangor. You don't want that, do you? You never know what could happen to a woman like her in a place like that. She could be killed or raped. You wouldn't want her to spend even a single night there, would you?" Lily was grasping but could think of nothing else to say. Maybe the mention of Natalie's family would bring her back to herself, make her see reason.

The girl stood, and a laugh bubbled out of her. "This is Plan B," she said, her words slurred. "Plan A was Antonio coming over to take your statement, you know, the one where you confess to killing your sister. I've been paying him to do my bidding. But let's be honest, I kinda knew

Plan A wasn't gonna pan out. Plan B is more exciting and *dramatic*." She gestured toward Antonio's body and waved a dismissive hand. "Don't worry about him. He was a shitty cop anyway."

Natalie took the bottles of alcohol out of her satchel. Each was plugged with a rag. Liquid dripped from the bottoms of the soaked fabric.

With the gun on the floor in front of her, Natalie eyed Lily as she took a lighter from her pocket and teasingly held it up for Lily to see. A tight smile lit her face as she flicked it, and all at once, a long flame appeared, dancing and dangerous.

"What are you doing?" Lily's voice rose with panic.

Natalie threw her a look of annoyance. "What do you think I'm doing?"

"If you set the cabin on fire, you'll die too. This whole place is made of wood. For God's sake, it'll be engulfed by flames in minutes."

She threw Lily a look of incredulousness. "That's Plan B." Then she held the flame to a wick. It lit instantly. For a moment, she studied it, looking at it from different angles, fascinated, then catapulted the bottle against a wall. It exploded on impact, licks of flames shot up, catching the curtains, and small pools of liquor burned in dozens of spots on the tinder-dry floorboards. Another landed in the kitchen on the mat in front of the sink. Flames flared up as high as the ceiling, and shards of glass sprayed down like ice pellets.

Natalie held a third bottle, ready to light it. "This one's for you." There was a smile in her voice.

No time, no thought, no fear. Lily ran at Natalie, knocking the homemade bomb from her hands before she had a chance to light it. The girl fell backward, hitting the hard stone of the fireplace, but gained back her feet in seconds. With hands entwined in Lily's hair, she smashed her head downward with a mighty thrust, toward an upraised knee. The sharp crack of cartilage echoed in Lily's head, and pain seared her brain.

Blackness fell.

Natalie slid to the floor, her legs rubbery, her energy spent. She leaned against the wooden column between the living room and kitchen. The flames were spreading quickly, engulfing furniture now. They were pretty, so pretty, she thought in amazement as the heat and the pills lulled her into contentment.

She saw the dog flee upstairs to the loft, instinct driving him to a safer place, at least for the moment. Soon there would be no such thing as a safe place.

It was hot. Hot as hell, and Natalie yanked off her hat and tried to remove her jacket, fighting with it as it twisted and tangled in muddled-up arms that didn't do what she wanted them to. She took the pills from her jacket pocket, then tossed her winter gear into the flames. Everything was right with the world. Justice had been done, and soon her pain would be over. No more worrying about her parents fighting, wondering when they were going to divorce and leave her, or be hauled off to prison. No more loneliness. No more disrespect. People would remember her now, know what she was capable of. She'd wait just a bit longer, enjoy the moment, and wonder at the beauty of the fire raging around her, then she'd down what was left of the pills and drift off. Her death would be painless. Just a calm, deep slumber.

Lily lay a few feet away, a puddle of crimson pooled around her head, but the sputtering coughs and labored breaths told Natalie she wasn't yet dead. Smoke was filling the cabin, but the openness of the high, vaulted ceilings provided plenty of room for it to rise. Natalie still had time to enjoy her handiwork.

Aiden was sprawled on the couch, and she had no idea if he was still among the living, though she doubted it. Flames licked at the edges of the area rug near the sofa he was on. The fire would get him first. She didn't really mind, but it would have been nicer if Lily was the first to go. That way Natalie would be certain to see her struggle to breathe her last. She would have even dragged her closer to the flames if the pills hadn't stolen her energy.

Her eyelids were made of lead and she let them close. Just for a moment.

CHAPTER 32

Get up NOW! a voice screamed in Aiden's brain, three little words bursting with panic. A sudden urgency washed over him, and with difficulty, he opened his eyes but wanted to shut them again just a second later. They were leaden and burned to close. He was tired, so tired.

"Hurry!" It was a woman's voice.

Lily's face filled the screen of his imagination, and along with it came a sense of dread, this time so strong it set his heart to hammering. He opened his eyes again, and now he saw that the cabin was in flames. The heat of the blaze came at him in waves, stealing his breath. Panic lurched him to his feet, and smoke clogged his nostrils.

Not far off in the hazy distance he saw a woman standing alone, staring at him. He didn't know her, or did he? "She needs you," she demanded.

It sounded like Lily, but he knew it wasn't her. This woman was smaller. "Sara?" he choked out.

A flicker of a smile played on her lips as if in reply. She spoke again. "Help her." Then the smoky haze engulfed the woman and she was gone.

Aiden waved away the smoke in an attempt to glimpse her again. It was no use; she'd either moved away farther into the thick blackness or vanished completely. Dizziness nearly felled him, but he managed to grab the back of the sofa, steadying his totter. The floor was a furnace, burning the bottoms of his bare feet. He pushed the pain away and waved off the smoke in front of him, which he noticed, thankfully, was rising.

There was a blanket wrapped around his midsection. No, he thought, not wrapped, *stuck*. He realized, with horror, it was his own blood making it adhere to the bare skin of his torso. He'd been shot! He remembered that now. It all came back. Natalie holding the gun, aiming it at him; him not believing she would or *could* shoot him; him thinking he'd talk her out of whatever crazy idea she was entertaining.

With trembling fingers, he peeled the blood-soaked blanket away and peered down at the hole in his side. Blood bubbled from it, oozing and pulsing with each beat of his heart. Pain in his shoulder sent his fingers exploring gingerly until they grazed another hole.

There was nothing he could do to help himself, and he knew with heart-rending finality that time was not on his side. He willed himself calm and set out to find Lily.

A man lying prone on the floor caught his attention. He moved close enough to get a better look. "Jesus

Christ!" Deputy Deluca's head was haloed with a spray of crimson. In his hand lay his cell phone. With an agonizing rip of pain, Aiden fell to his knees. No way the man could be alive, but he checked for a pulse anyway. Finding none, he took the phone and punched in 911. A voice on the other end asked what the emergency was.

Smoke caught in his throat, making him sputter. "Need an ambulance and fire truck. Cabin on Ryan's Road. Hurry."

An urge came over him just then—to sit or maybe lie down, his energy spent, as if uttering just a few words had taken all he had left. He'd take a little rest and wait for the ambulance. It wouldn't be long. Help would be there soon.

Slowly, as he went the short distance from kneeling to sitting, he saw Natalie. He inched nearer, until he was close enough to see her eyes were closed.

Smoke burned his eyes and throat. His world was growing dim, then the sound of a cough startled him back to consciousness. "Lily?" he called, pressing the blanket over his nose and mouth to keep the smoke from his lungs. His vision blurred, focusing in and out like the lens of a camera. He was dying; he wanted to die. The thought of moving even just another foot was akin to climbing Mount Everest.

"In front of you." It was the voice again. Sara's voice. This is no hallucination, he told himself. He lay prone, stretching himself out, hands searching, sweeping across the floor until finally, with great relief, they fell on the woman he loved. He felt the silk of her hair and stroked it. "Lily?"

Her head moved ever so slightly. A nod, he realized. She was nodding.

"I...I...called for help." He coughed and held a palm to his side to stem the flow of blood. With each hack, it oozed through his fingers. How much time did he have left? How much blood had he lost? His world was growing more dreamlike. Was any of this really happening?

He couldn't stand and was growing weaker by the second. Lifting her would be impossible. There was no hope. He might as well take her in his arms and lie beside her. Together they would wait for whichever came first, rescue or death.

Suddenly, it was as if a pair of hands were on him, trying in vain to pull him to his feet. "Save her," the voice demanded.

But how could he possibly get Lily to safety? The voice was wrong. There was nothing he could do. Aiden clasped Lily's hand, entwining his fingers with hers.

"I love you," she whispered.

* * *

A blast of frigid air assaulted him like a slap to the face, and Aiden gulped it in greedily. Choking and sputtering, his breaths came in wild, frantic waves, filling him with a momentary panic. Would he ever breathe again? A chilled hand lay across his forehead, calming him. "Sara?" He looked around, but saw no one.

Smoke streamed from the open cabin door, and he was shocked to realize he was outside, lying in sooty snow. Lily was behind him, a little farther away from the blaze.

He elbowed to her side and saw that her nose was smashed flat, and was not just broken, but crushed. Blood had already begun to dry and congeal thickly around her nostrils. He did his best to check for gunshot wounds. There was no growing ring of red oozing through her clothing. Thankfully, he didn't think she'd been shot. But her face! Her poor broken face. What had that bitch done to her? His pulse quickened as his anger rose. Let the flames take her. Let that fucking girl die and go straight to hell.

"Lily." He shook her shoulders with what little strength he had left. "Wake up."

Her eyes fluttered open and a hand flew to her ruined face. Tears flowed, cutting trenches through her soot-covered cheeks, and she let out a ragged breath. "Oh, God."

The sound of twigs breaking and snow crunching beneath the weight of something small caught Aiden's attention. Rex ambled toward them, dirty and shivering. He turned in a circle and curled up between them. Lily was safe; his job was done. He closed his eyes and let the last of his energy drain away.

CHAPTER 33

Hospitals were loud places. The beeps and buzzes and the sound of trolleys being pushed along the hallway had kept Lily up most of the night, along with the constant intrusions of the nurses stopping by to take vitals, or change an empty saline bag. But somewhere along the way, sleep claimed her, and she'd had the most amazing dream. At least she *thought* it was a dream. It had been so real. Coming back to waking life was harsh and unwelcomed, because in her dream, Mrs. G. had come to see her. Could be the pain meds, but that didn't explain the authenticity of it.

In the "dream," Mrs. G. was sitting beside her on the hospital bed. The weight of the woman made Lily's legs slide toward her. How peculiar to dream something so precisely. Then her friend took her hand and kissed it, in much the same way Lily had done with hers not that long ago.

"Angel, you're going to be just fine," the old woman said, only she wasn't old. Lily *knew* it was Mrs. G., but she looked thirty-something. The same jet-black hair framed a pretty, delicate face. However, her complexion was no longer a stark contrast to the pallor she'd developed in her later years, but olive and sun bronzed. Her hair too, was thicker and longer. Eyes shining with the brightness of youth stared down at Lily.

"What are you doing here?" Lily asked.

"Just came for a visit."

"Will you be staying a while?"

"No, angel, I can't. I came to thank you for being so kind to me over the years, for being my friend, and to tell you that fella you brought to meet me the other night, well, he's a nice young man. Good looking too. You'll be happy together."

Mrs. G. smiled and Lily saw straight white teeth, not the dentures time had yellowed. She was about to ask how she managed to come see her. After all, Mrs. G. wasn't in the best of health. And how did she know she and Aiden would be happy together? She sounded so certain.

Before Lily could get the questions out, her friend began to fade. At first, she thought it a trick of the eye, but soon Lily saw the green-and-brown design of the curtain around her bed through the old woman's figure. She continued to dissolve, growing brighter yet more transparent by the second until, finally, all that was left was a small wheel of light that seemed to spin itself down an unseen drain. The soft echo of the word "good-bye" played in Lily's head.

Someone kissed her forehead. It was Mrs. G. come back to continue their visit, Lily thought with a spark of hope, but when she turned toward the kiss, she saw it had come from Annie.

Slowly, she shifted around to her friend. Her face was swollen and tender, her jaw stiff and sore but not broken. She'd been damn lucky.

"Hi. Sorry, didn't mean to startle you. You OK? Need anything?"

"No. I'm fine. Have you seen Aiden today?" Her words were slow and she mumbled because of the limited mobility of her jaw.

Annie set down a paper bag on the wheeled tray at the foot of Lily's bed and took out a cinnamon bun dripping with frosting, as well as a large coffee.

"I stopped in to see him before coming to visit you. The poor guy." She frowned.

Lily sighed. "It's just so hard being away from him." She picked at a piece of the bun and gingerly placed it in her mouth. Eating was an uncomfortable but necessary challenge, and the bun was a nice change from the soup and Jell-O diet she was on. She sipped her coffee, thinking nothing ever tasted so good.

Annie laid a gentle hand on Lily's arm, her brow furrowed. "I have some news and I'm afraid it's not good."

"What is it?"

"I'm sorry, hon, but your friend from the center, Mrs. G., passed away last night. Gail called the diner first thing this morning."

Relief washed over Lily, not grief or sadness. A smile played on her lips as her eyes met Annie's. "I already knew about Mrs. G., and it's OK. I know she's fine now. She's in a better place."

Annie cocked her head and grinned. "Really? How did you—"

"Let's just say it's a long story."

She splayed a hand over her heart. "You have no idea how relieved I am. The last thing I wanted was to add to your troubles. Rex is doing well. He's happy at my place," Annie said. "I just might not give him back. He's so sweet."

"Thank you for taking care of him, Annie. You're a great friend."

"Too bad about Natalie though."

Lily huffed a sigh of displeasure. "Don't know how I feel about that. Is it awful a part of me wished she'd died? I know it's horrible she's burned so badly, but the anger I feel toward that girl... I don't know if it'll ever go away." Lily gave her head a slow shake. "She shot Antonio right in front of me, Annie. I saw his brains splatter on the wall, the back of his head blown right off, and then there's what she did to Aiden."

"Shhh. Hush. I'm sorry for bringing her up. Last thing I want is to upset you. She's a very disturbed girl. What she did wasn't just wrong, it was despicable."

A rap at the door caught their attention. Sheriff Wilkins stood, hat in hand, in the entranceway. "OK if I come in?"

Lily nodded, not sure how she felt about visiting with Wilkins. Seemed there were a lot of uncertainties in her life at the moment.

Annie got up. "I'll leave you two alone. Your cell phone's right there beside you, Lily. Call me if you need anything. Best I get back to the diner anyway. Denise is probably having a nervous breakdown by now."

Annie kissed Lily on the cheek. "I'll be by in the morning to pick you up."

Wilkins stepped into the room as Annie exited.

"Mind if I sit?" he asked, lowering himself into the plastic chair beside her. The tall, lanky man placed his hat at the foot of the bed and then leaned forward and clasped his hands. "So, how you feelin'? Any pain? Need me to getcha anythin'?"

"Not so good but better than Aiden, I imagine." Her tone was bitter.

"Yup, I suppose so." He cleared his throat. "I stopped by to see how you're doing and, well, to say sorry. I put you through a hell of a time." Wilkins shook his head. "Us lawmen are a special breed, always followin' our noses and going where the evidence takes us. I shoulda known better than to suspect you, Lily, but when your daddy left all that money to Sara and nothing to you, I had to put myself in your shoes. Hell, if my dad did that to me and my brother, I'd be spitting mad. And Antonio, rest his soul, had me convinced it was you." He ran a hand over his day's worth of scruff. "Damn, in all the years I've been sheriff, I've never lost a deputy in the line of duty. Hell of a loss."

A throb began in Lily's temples. She had to tell Wilkins the truth about Deluca. No sense in waiting. After a deep breath, she began, "Sheriff, seeing Deputy Deluca get shot is a sight that will never leave my mind, but he wasn't the man you think he was. Natalie told me she'd been paying him off and that he was doing her bidding. She killed him because she had no more use for him."

His head turned, almost in slow motion, his eyes growing wide and his mouth falling open like a gate on a busted hinge. "No. I don't believe it."

"Think about it. Natalie had just killed Deluca and shot Aiden. She was planning on killing me and then taking her own life. What did she have to lose? She was telling the truth." Lily expected a reaction, but he sat still as a statue, gaze fixed on the wall in front of him.

Finally he spoke. "I've worked side by side with Antonio for years. I know he didn't make a helluva lot of money, but he didn't have a wife and kids to support. He had plenty to live on. Why would he do such a thing?" Wilkins shook his head in disbelief.

To Lily, the answer was simple. "Greed."

He threw his hands up in a shrug. "I knew the man. Trusted him. I never thought he'd do something like that."

Lily let her gaze fall to her hands and said, "You knew me too and for a lot longer than you knew Deputy Deluca. Still, you thought I was capable of murdering my own sister."

Wilkins dropped his head into his hands. Long, thin fingers rubbed at his temples. "You're right." He sighed and looked up at her. "How careless I've been and how stupid!"

Damn right, she wanted to say, but bit her tongue.

"There's more."

Wilkins's eyes widened before he got to his feet and began to pace in a small orbit at the foot of her bed. "Tell me."

Lily took a deep breath then blew it out. "You'd better drop the murder charges against Gabrielle Lyons as soon as possible, sheriff. She didn't kill my sister. Natalie did."

Wilkins stopped pacing and stared down at her. He couldn't have looked more shocked if red ants were marching from her ears. He opened his mouth to speak, then shut it again, jerked away from her as if he was about to leave, then turned back. "Why do we have a murder weapon with Gabrielle Lyons's prints on it?"

"I don't know, but Natalie made it crystal clear she was the one who shot Sara. She confessed to me and was more than happy to do so."

"You sure she wasn't just trying to protect her mother?"

"Absolutely not. It still gives me chills thinking of the joy in her eyes when she told me she killed my sister. She was happy to be torturing me with the truth."

He sat back down. "Shit," was all he said for several seconds. Then, "To tell you the truth, I have to admit I was shocked about Gabrielle's prints being on that gun." He heaved a sigh. "I gotta say it again, Lily. I'm so sorry. I really am."

"It was frustrating that no one believed me. That was the hardest part." She kept her voice even, not allowing the emotion bubbling under the surface to rise.

"I know. I know." His head bobbed furiously as if in time to some unheard song.

"No, you couldn't possibly know, sheriff. I'm pretty much a pariah in this town. This town where I've lived since I was twelve. This town where I own a business and used to have friends. Now, I can count the number of friends I still have on one hand." Despite her resolve, tears began to well in her eyes, threatening to fall.

He looked at her sheepishly, then reached behind him for the small square box of one-ply tissue sitting on a counter and placed it on the tray in front of her.

Lily plucked out a few to blot her eyes.

Wilkins dared to let a small smile play on his lips. "I did do one thing right though." He waited a beat, then said, "I hired Aiden."

She didn't understand. Yes, he'd hired him, but all that did was get Aiden shot. She threw Wilkins a puzzled look.

He shifted uncomfortably in his seat once he realized Lily hadn't gotten his meaning and said, "If Aiden hadn't come to town, the two of you never woulda met. Guess I'm a better matchmaker than I am a sheriff."

That made Lily smile and prompted her to ask, "How is Aiden? You've got to know more than I do. *Please* don't spare my feelings. I need to know if he's going to be OK."

"I've got an idea. Be back in a minute." Wilkins loped out of the room and not thirty seconds later was back pushing a wheelchair. "How 'bout I take you to see him?"

Aiden's hospital room was bright, Lily noticed. It was a double, but he had the whole thing to himself, no roommate for the time being. He was lying in the bed nearest the window.

"Do you think he's asleep?" she whispered to Wilkins.

"Don't know."

He wheeled her closer and Lily was disappointed to see Aiden's eyes were shut. She tried to push herself up out of the chair, but the sheriff kept her in it with a gentle hand on her shoulder. "I'll bring you closer, Lily. No need to get up."

Now she was at Aiden's bedside and reached out to smooth his tousled hair. His facial hair had grown from scruff to a beard, and she wished she could take care of him. Clean him up, make him look more like himself.

Still, she was surprised how strong and capable he looked even lying in a hospital bed. Even with machines beside him—the IV, the oxygen mask—he still looked indestructible. How had he managed to save her? Aiden O'Rourke was no ordinary man in her eyes. He was Superman.

"Aiden," Lily whispered, unsure whether or not to wake him. There was no response, just the beeping of machines and the sounds of business as usual out in the hall.

Wilkins pulled up a chair for himself. "I sure don't like hospitals. All them machines beepin' and the smell. I don't know what it is. Disinfectant? Death?"

Lily looked at him wide-eyed, surprised at his choice of words.

"Sorry," he said quickly. "I wasn't implying Aiden's gonna die. Hell, Lily, he's built like a Mac truck. If anyone can come through this, it's him. I knew it the minute I saw him. He's one tough son of a gun."

Aiden turned his head toward them, eyes still shut. Lily inched to the edge of the wheelchair and took his hand, caressing it. She yearned to be close enough to kiss him.

"Lily?" Aiden's voice was barely a whisper.

"Yes, yes, I'm here."

His eyes opened and she thought she saw a smile under the oxygen mask. "You OK?" His words were barely audible, a tin-can echo.

"Got a couple of shiners, sore jaw, swollen face and who knows what my nose is going to end up looking like, but yeah, otherwise I'm fine. How are you feeling? Do you need anything?"

He shook his head. "I'll live."

Wilkins stood and looked down on him. "Sorry you had to go through all this, Aiden. The department is at your disposal. You just holler if you need anything."

"Just take care of my girl," Aiden said before his lids closed again.

CHAPTER 34

Lily felt pretty good considering she'd been in the hospital for three days. But she didn't want to go home just yet.

"I wanna see Aiden then we'll go, OK?"

Annie shrugged. "All right then, come on."

Aiden was sitting up; one of the machines he'd been hooked up to the day before was now gone. He was left with an oxygen tube hugging his nostrils and an IV stand with a couple of bags hanging from it. A young nurse stood at his bedside, jotting something down on a clipboard. She smiled when she saw Lily and Annie. "Don't tell me. You must be Lily. Aiden's told me all about you," she said, throwing Aiden a wink.

"Yes," Lily answered, but her eyes were on Aiden.

He was clean-shaven, and his hair was combed back from his face. He smiled and there was that cavernous dimple. It was funny just how much she loved it. It somehow made Aiden, Aiden. As if he'd be someone else without it.

"How's he doing?" Lily asked.

"Just needs lots of rest and to take it easy for a while." The nurse turned to replace a saline bag. "He's quite the hero around town. Heard he saved you from a burning building then even went back in to get your dog. All that with two bullet holes in him." She laughed. "Impressive. Anyway, I'll get out of your way. I'm sure he wants to visit with you."

The nurse replaced the clipboard at the end of Aiden's bed, and then Lily heard the soft squeak of her rubber-soled shoes as she left.

"You all ready to go home?" Aiden asked, spying Annie with Lily's bag.

"Not without seeing you first. You look so handsome. Don't tell me that young nurse gave you a sponge bath." She winked.

Aiden laughed and held his side. The laugh quickly morphed into a cough. "Sorry. They told me to sit up as much as I can to clear my lungs. Seems I'm coughing a lot these days." He waved at Annie, who was standing behind Lily. "Thanks for all you're doing, Annie."

"No problemo." She placed Lily's bag on the ground in front of her. "How 'bout I go get us some coffee? You allowed to have a coffee, Aiden?"

"Better make it apple juice for me."

Annie left and Lily took a seat. "No sponge bath then?"

"Unfortunately not. They forced me to get up this morning and walk around a bit. Hurt like hell, but they won't let me go home until everything is working." He looked slightly embarrassed.

Lily smiled and bent to kiss his cheek. "So, when can you go home?"

He gave her a hesitant look, as if not wanting to answer. Then she realized his home had burned to the ground. Her hand flew to her chest. "Oh, God. I'm sorry. Guess I should rephrase that—when can you come to *my* home?"

He raised a brow. "You want me to stay with you?"

"Of course." She was about to say, Where else could you go? but stopped herself, realizing it might be a bit harsh.

"Well, I don't have much to pack, so, sure, if you'll have me, I'd love to stay with you."

Pack? She knew it was a joke since all his belongings had been lost in the fire, but just that word, that one tiny word, made her think of him leaving town.

"I didn't know if you still wanted me in your life after what happened. I should have done more to protect you, but I didn't think Natalie was going to…to do what she did. I thought she was just a mixed-up kid, and I could talk her down off that ledge she seemed to be on. I'm so sorry, Lily."

She slipped a careful arm around him and kissed his neck and then his lips. "You *saved* me, for real this time. How can you say you didn't do enough? Without your help, I wouldn't be alive." And we wouldn't be together, she wanted to say, but were they together? She didn't know the answer to that question and was afraid to raise the issue. Time would tell. She'd have to be patient.

He pressed his eyes shut and shook his head, leaving her bewildered.

CHAPTER 35

Lily's follow-up appointment with the surgeon wasn't for a couple more weeks, but today was the day she was allowed to remove the bandages from her face.

Her stomach fluttered with butterflies, excitement and worry giving them life. What would Aiden do if she wasn't as pretty as before? Probably still love her, she thought with relief.

She took a seat on the edge of the tub and squeezed her eyes shut. "OK, go ahead. Be gentle," she said to Aiden. She could feel his smile even though she couldn't see it. He'd been released from the hospital two days ago and seemed to be doing well. Still on painkillers, of course, though Lily noticed he hardly took them. He said the abdominal wound was uncomfortable and gave him trouble when he sat or got up, but surprisingly, it was his shoulder that hurt most.

Lily felt Aiden picking at the edge of one of the white steri-strips that lay across her nose and cheeks. The skin around her eyes was still black in spots, but a yellow cast had come in beneath it.

He carefully pulled up the edges on another strip. "You OK?"

Lily nodded. She heard Rex come in and felt him lie on the scatter mat at her feet. Canine moral support, she supposed.

Aiden finally had one strip off completely, then another and after another minute, the last one.

"How do I look?"

"Beautiful." Aiden handed her a mirror and smiled hugely at her. *He* looked the same, his dimple, his days' worth of scruff, that black tousled hair. How he looked so good after nearly dying, she had no idea, and secretly prayed her nose wouldn't be a smashed-up mess.

She took the mirror from him with shaky hands and immediately started to cry when she saw her reflection. "I'm ugly."

Aiden's smile went out and he looked around for a tissue. Finding none, he grabbed a wad of toilet paper and handed it to her, all the while trying to hold his arm and shoulder as still as possible. "It's still a bit swollen, but I can tell it's going to be fine. Your nose will look exactly like it did before," he reassured her.

She held the mirror up again and turned her head slightly this way and that to examine the doctor's handiwork from every direction. There were no stitches. She was thankful for that. They were all on the inside, she'd been told, in order to prevent scarring. After another look, she decided Aiden might be right. Maybe once the swelling and bruising went away, it wouldn't be so bad after all. Of course, the bruising would go, but it was hard to imagine the swollen tissue shrunk back to its original shape and form. She handed back the mirror. "Hope you're right."

"It's gonna take some time before we're both a hundred percent." Aiden sat beside her and hugged her to him. "We're falling apart, aren't we?" He laughed and held his side as he did. "But we've got each other and that's all that counts."

Did they really have each other, she wondered, and if so, for how long? True, he had told her he loved her, but it had been a while since Aiden said anything about their future or whether he was even staying in town. The force of that worry was so strong, she had to push it away, and couldn't yet bring herself to ask him about it. Besides, she didn't want anything to ruin the time they had together, no matter how long or short. "Thank you," she said and smiled. "You make me feel beautiful and special no matter what."

He gave her face a gentle caress. "No need to thank me. What I say and do for you comes easy because it's from my heart. You're doing the same for me, remember?"

His touch awakened her desire, and his words only strengthened it. She stood and took his hand, leading him into the bedroom. They stopped at the foot of the bed. Aiden pulled her close and peppered soft, feathery kisses on her forehead, her eyelids, her nose then, more hungrily, her mouth.

Lily undid the buttons of his shirt, one at a time, slowly, carefully, mindful of his injuries. She bent to kiss his stomach, just above the packing over his wound. Aiden was unable yet to don jeans or any kind of pants that fastened with a zipper and button. Lily eased off the pajama bottoms he was wearing.

With a sly smile, Aiden eased himself into the bed then pulled up the covers for her. Lily slid in beside him and they lay facing each other, caressing, kissing, touching. Even though she knew he wanted her badly, and she wanted him just as much, being so close, so intimate, had to be enough for now. The feel of his heart beating against hers and the warmth of him was all she needed. They lay together for a long time, silently enjoying each other until sleep finally came for them.

* * *

"Do you think about Natalie?" Lily asked Aiden over breakfast the next morning. It was the first time either of them had brought up her name since the night at the cabin when all hell had broken loose.

Aiden looked thoughtful, as if choosing his words carefully, then replied simply, "Can't get her out of my head."

Lily sipped her coffee and took a bite of her bagel. Eating was still a bit of a chore, but the pain lessened with each passing day. "Me neither. For the longest time, it was as if everything that happened that night was just a bad dream."

Aiden's eyes widened with her words. "I know what you mean. It *was* surreal and...well, never mind."

Lily smiled halfheartedly. "What were you going to say?"

He shook his head and waved a dismissive hand. "That's a story for another time."

Her cell phone rang. Coaxing out whatever Aiden was about to say could wait.

It was Sheriff Wilkins. He'd called out of courtesy to let her know Natalie's doctors cleared her for questioning. Lily eyed Aiden. "Will you be OK alone for a while?"

* * *

"She's got a visitor right now. I'm sorry, you'll have to come back another time," the plump nurse said to Lily.

"Yes, I know. Sheriff Wilkins is in there with Natalie, questioning her. He's expecting me." She'd gathered up all of her confidence and injected it into her voice.

"I wasn't aware anyone else was coming." The nurse planted her hands on well-padded hips and examined Lily through narrowed eyes. "Wait here." She pushed open the slate-gray door to Natalie's room and was back within seconds, trailed by Wilkins, who was decked out in what looked to Lily like a hazmat suit.

He pulled down the surgical mask he was wearing. "Lily?" Then turned to the nurse. "Give us a second."

When she was out of earshot, Wilkins took Lily by the shoulder and pulled her closer. "I only told you I'd be questioning Natalie out of courtesy. I didn't expect you to turn up here." His voice was a furious whisper.

"I'm here now and I think you owe it to me to let me come in there with you."

"No way."

"She's allowed visitors now, right? So, I'm here for a visit." When he didn't answer, she continued, "I can help. Seeing me might unnerve her, get her to say more." She waited a beat or two. Still no answer. "How long have you been questioning her?"

He spoke finally. "Just got here and I barely got started when you showed up. Her parents are on their way. I don't have much time. They've got her some big-city lawyer. If I don't get in there now, that lawyer will have her shut up like a bank vault in no time."

Lily took hold of his arm. "We'd better hurry up then." But Wilkins stood as solid as a statue, unyielding and firm. She couldn't budge him.

"No. I can't let you go in there."

"After what you and your department, not to mention Natalie, put me through, I'm going through that door whether you like it or not." Something in her glare must have told Wilkins just how serious she was, because he waved the nurse back over with a sigh of exasperation.

"Miss Valier will be coming in too," he said.

"All right, you'll have to put these on." The nurse pointed to a stack of coveralls. "Masks and gloves are over there on the counter. It's a sterile environment, so you'll not be allowed to take them off. Understand? She's a very sick young lady, and we can't risk infection."

"Is she in pain?" Lily asked. Although she despised Natalie, a small part of her felt sorry for the girl.

"She's got third-degree burns over forty percent of her body, but she's on a morphine drip so she's comfortable."

"She going to be in here a long time?"

"Yes, months I'm afraid," the nurse answered with pursed lips and a slow shake of her head.

Lily steeled herself for what she was going to see when she walked through the door in front of her.

"Looks like you have another visitor," the nurse announced, nodding for Lily and Wilkins to enter, then took her leave.

Lily made her way into the large private room. There were no plants or flowers or cards. Sterile room, she remembered.

Natalie was on her back, the bed inclined slightly. No blankets or sheets touched the damaged parts of her from what Lily could see, just moist dressings. Her bed was surrounded by a thick sheet of plastic, which Lily surmised was a barrier between the girl and the germ-filled world around her.

As she moved farther into the room, she noticed Natalie's hair was singed to the scalp in several places. Red, raw patches of blistering skin gave her scalp a checkerboard appearance, but her face seemed to have been spared the same fate. It wasn't until she drew nearer that Lily spied an angry splotch at the bottom of Natalie's jawline.

An IV drip and heart monitor did their jobs, and a small TV hung from a wall-mounted arm beside her, inside the confines of the plastic housing.

"Knew you'd show up sooner or later," Natalie said, her eyes sleep heavy. "Don't worry, I'm going to prison when I get out of here. Right, Sheriff Wilkins?" Her words were slow and it seemed an effort for her to speak.

Wilkins didn't reply but Lily did. "I'd say there's a damn good chance of that."

A small groan escaped the girl as she tried to lift her head. "Can't see much with that mask on. Your face messed up?"

Lily thought she saw a smile curl the girl's lips. "I'm just fine," she replied.

Natalie seemed to lose interest and turned her head to the muted TV. Lily saw a morning talk show on the small screen. A pretty blonde woman smiled and talked animatedly to her co-host. This made Lily want to grab hold of Natalie and shake her, to pull her attention back to her. Instead, she asked, "Are you sorry for what you did?"

Wilkins grabbed her wrist in warning, but she was undeterred and yanked away from him. "You murdered two people and an unborn baby! I'd like to know what's going on in that head of yours. Do you even comprehend what you've done?"

Natalie turned back slowly and glared. "Now my outside matches my inside."

This wasn't what she was expecting. Were there tears in the girl's eyes? Lily thought there might be. She was about to say she deserved everything she was going to get. That a life sentence in a maximum-security prison wasn't good enough, that she should be sentenced to death.

"You done now? I've got a job to do," Wilkins said to Lily. He'd left her now and was standing by the window, resting against the ledge, arms crossed over his narrow chest.

She threw a glance his way, lips pursed, then turned back to Natalie. "Why did you try to kill me?"

"Because women like *you* get everything you want." Tears now streamed down her cheeks, and she let them come and did not wipe them away. "You'll never be alone in this world because you're beautiful."

Jealousy? Lily remembered her talk with Aiden about what jealousy could drive a person to do. Only they'd been talking about Gabrielle at the time, not Natalie. Never had she thought Natalie wanted her dead because she was jealous of her. It seemed such a weak, childish reason.

There was a part in the plastic sheeting and Lily pushed her way through. Even with the mask on, she could smell the girl—dead flesh and whatever medication was soaked into the dressings made her stomach lurch. How on earth anyone could be a nurse was beyond her. She summoned up more steel.

"And you thought ruining the lives of others would solve your self-esteem issues?" Her voice rose with the words. There was the slap of the thick plastic sheets being moved apart, and Wilkins was beside her now. But he was silent and not scolding, and this surprised Lily.

Natalie took hold of her morphine pump and dosed herself to the max. Her features relaxed immediately as the drug-induced calm enveloped her. "I didn't mean to kill Sara." She smiled and looked up at Wilkins. "That caught your attention? You think I'm going to spill my guts now?"

"Natalie, just remember what you say now can and will be used in a court of law—"

The girl looked annoyed. "You already read me my rights. Don't really give a shit what happens to me now, anyway. My life's over." Her words were beginning to slur.

Lily burned with agitation. Why had Wilkins interfered? Natalie might have gone on and told her why she'd killed Sara. Stupid move, sheriff, she wanted to say but only huffed. "What were you going to say?" she asked Natalie.

Natalie yawned and rubbed an eye with the heel of her hand. "Can't we talk later?"

Lily slapped a palm hard against the wall behind Natalie's head. Her arm vibrated with the force of it right up to her shoulder. Wilkins jumped and Natalie's eyes widened. "Goddamn it. Tell me." Her voice was a growl.

"Easy," Wilkins whispered and narrowed his eyes at Lily. But she turned from him and set her eyes once again on Natalie.

The bravado seemed to slip from the girl, and her expression changed to one of resignation. With downcast eyes, she began, "I went to your sister's just to talk.

Thought I could make her understand how she was hurting my family, and asked her to leave us be." She looked up at Lily then, her eyes brimming with tears. "She could have gone anywhere and started a new life. I don't know why she was so set on ruining mine. We argued. I saw the gun lying on her kitchen counter, and before I realized what I was doing, I was aiming it at her." The girl's words were coming slowly now, and Lily feared the medication was about to take her away.

"And then?" Wilkins coaxed.

Tears spilled. "I shot her in the throat. Didn't know what to do, so I ran. Took the gun with me. My mother was going to divorce my dad. Couldn't take the constant fighting, my dad not coming home. I missed having a family to make me feel safe. Can you understand that?"

Lily did understand, more than she cared to admit.

Natalie's eyes closed, and Lily shook her back to consciousness. "But why try to pin it on me?" The girl jolted and her head wobbled like a seed-laden sunflower on its stalk. "'Cause I didn't like you...and it was Deluca's idea. I went to him for help. He knew about the inheritance money and said it could be a motive for you wanting your sister dead." She sighed, deep and heavy, then continued in a slow staccato, "He told me my dad would be the prime suspect and if I gave him a little money now and then, he could convince the sheriff you did it."

Wilkins had his notebook out and was writing furiously. "Why does the murder weapon have your mother's prints on it?"

"Probably found it under my bed. Mother never cleans, but she does snoop, a lot. I'm so tired...don't want to talk anymore."

It seemed Natalie was asleep within seconds, and Lily crept closer and peered down at her. Blood and pus-soaked dressings covered the girl's right side. Despite wanting to turn away, Lily forced herself to take it in. Competing emotions battled within her. Yes, Natalie was young, barely a woman, but she'd done so much damage to the lives of so many. Still, no matter how long Natalie spent in prison, her scarred body would remind her of the suffering she'd caused. With that thought, anger flowed away and pity replaced it.

"Guess you got what you needed, huh?" Lily said to Wilkins.

He nodded his reply.

CHAPTER 36

Six months later

Aiden looked over at Lily. She was as radiant as ever. Her face had healed perfectly, not so much as a bruise remained. He, on the other hand, was still on the mend but doing much better, especially with the help of Lily's ever-present nurturing.

She was sitting in their booth at the diner, looking out the window at the sun setting on a bright April day. It took some coaxing to get her to close up shop early, but he'd managed. Lily Valier was set in her ways. He turned the "Open" sign to "Closed," and it brought a smile to him when he thought back to how he once saw her as a hard nut to crack. Turned out she wasn't really. Lily was tender and sweet, and the walls she'd built up around her, he knew now, were constructed out of a need for self-preservation.

"You sure you know what you're doing?" she called.

Aiden was by the grill now, doing his best to whip up something edible. "No worries. I've got it all under control." Thankfully, Annie had helped by getting everything ready for him. All he had to do was throw the patties on the grill and push the start button on the microwave.

After uncorking a bottle of Shiraz, something he was good at, Aiden took it over to the table. He'd dressed up the chipped Arborite with a white linen tablecloth and a couple of candles in crystal holders. He lit them and filled their glasses. Lily lifted hers to her lips and sipped.

Aiden hurried back to the sound of meat sizzling on the grill.

"I really don't mind helping," she called after him.

"Order's almost up. Just sit there and look pretty." He threw her a smile and a wink.

Minutes later, he placed their meals on the table, a hamburger with a side of mashed potatoes.

Lily laughed. "Oh my God! The same meal you had on our first date!" She took a second to look it over. "This actually looks good."

They enjoyed their dinner and sipped their wine, and when they were done, Aiden took Lily's hands. "There's something I want to share with you that you might think is crazy."

Her eyes widened. "What is it?"

He took a deep breath. "Um, I really don't know how to begin."

"Just say it." She tightened her hold on his hand. "You can tell me anything."

He coughed then cleared his throat. There was no way around it. He was going to have to barrel right into what he needed to say or he'd never be able to tell her. "All right." He swallowed hard, then continued, "The night when, well, when Natalie tried to kill us. Um…I had some help saving you and apparently Rex too."

Her brow knit together and she cocked her head. "Huh?"

"I was woken up by a woman's voice. She said, 'Get up now' or something like that and told me you needed help. It was as if she was there beside me, yelling into my ear. I'd lost so much blood I could barely walk. All I managed to do was find you on the floor, but I knew there was no way I could carry you out of there. I called 911 on Deluca's cell phone and lay down beside you. I really thought we were going to die in that fire. The next thing I knew, we were both outside, then Rex came over, out of the bushes or someplace. For the life of me, Lily, I don't have a clue how he got out of the house. Or, for that matter, how *we* got out."

She was silent, starring at him, her mouth ajar.

"I think the woman…helped us." He looked her in the eyes, holding her gaze. "Is it crazy that I think she was your sister, Sara?"

Lily pulled her hands from his and they flew to her chest. Tears sprang to life and washed down her cheeks.

"I've been trying to figure this out since it happened, but I can't think of any other explanation. I saw her, Lily. I actually *saw* her and heard her voice just as if she was still alive. She looked a lot like you but shorter and with darker hair. I've seen those pictures in your office and, I swear, it looked just like her."

Finally, she found her voice. "Aiden, oh my God. I don't think you're crazy at all. What else did she say?" Her eyes were as round as silver dollars.

"Nothing really, just kept telling me to help you." He hung his head. "I did the best I could."

She took his hand again. "Yes, you did and you're no less my hero. What you've just shared brings me peace. You know I talk to Sara all the time, and I'm always looking around for her, hoping one day I'll catch a glimpse." She grinned, then reached across the table and caressed his stubbled cheek. "If you hadn't called for help, we'd be dead."

Aiden took Lily's hand and kissed it, then thumbed away her tears. A sigh of relief escaped him as he raked a hand through his hair. "I guess there's more to life than what we perceive with our senses. I never told you this, but I envied your faith, your belief in an afterlife. It's frightening to think this is all there is, but now I can honestly say that I think...no, not think...I *know* there is something beyond this life."

Lily's smile filled her face. "I'm happy to hear you say that. I just wish you'd told me sooner."

"I should have, but I needed time to reconcile it within myself. To figure things out." He stood, then dug into his pocket. "There's something else." Aiden looked down at Lily for a moment and smiled, then bent to one knee. "Lily Valier, I could say I love you with all my heart, but that would be a lie, because you *are* my heart. Without you I couldn't live because without you I wouldn't want to live.

"I love your smile and the way your eyes light up when you look at me. I love that you have more books than you do jewelry. I love your generosity and the way you bring joy to your friends at the seniors center. I love the way you kiss me because that's how I know you love me too.

"Like two halves of a whole, we were drawn to each other, coming together under the harshest of circumstances. But it was those circumstances that have taught me more about myself than I've learned over my lifetime. And you, you Lily, you've been an example of what a woman of character and integrity is. You're not only beautiful, you're…you're *perfection*. If you'll have me, I'd love to spend the rest of my life with you. Will you marry me?" He brought his hand around and in his palm was an old-fashioned, simple ring. A small diamond set in gold. No three-carat sparkler, that wasn't Lily's style.

A sharp intake of breath. "Oh my God! Yes, Aiden." She was on her feet, a smile a mile wide on her face. He slid the ring onto her finger. It fit as if it had been made for her. She brought it close to have a better look. "This was Mrs. G.'s. How did you…"

"Mrs. G. wanted you to have it. The night we visited, Gail took me aside and asked me outright if I was planning to propose. She said Mrs. G. willed it to you and when I told her I was, she said she'd hold onto it for me until I needed it."

Lily hugged him to her and sobbed into his shoulder. "It's perfect, Aiden. Perfect. I not only have you, but I have something to remember Mrs. G. by too. I'll think of her every time I look at it."

Suddenly a bustle of people clamored in through the front door, whistling and hollering their congratulations.

Lily looked at Aiden, surprise lighting her face. "You planned this?"

His smile broadened. "All your friends are here to help us celebrate."

Annie was first to hug and congratulate them, handing Lily a large bouquet of flowers, then Gail and Sharon from the seniors center. They had a cake with "Congratulations" written on it in big red letters, the vanilla frosting dotted with tiny fondant hearts.

Then Wilkins sauntered over, a bottle of champagne in hand, and slapped Aiden on the back. "You son of a gun. You got yourself the most beautiful woman in town. Congratulations!"

"I'm the lucky one," Lily said to Wilkins. "I've had a lot of loss in my life, but Aiden's given me more than I could *ever* ask for."

Wilkins smiled and gave Lily a peck on the cheek. "Glad you're happy. Really I am." Then he turned to Aiden. "We need a man like you in this town. I'll be retiring in a few months and now that I know you'll be sticking around, how would you like to be the new sheriff?"

Aiden's eyes lit up. "You serious?"

"As serious as this ulcer I've been nursing for the last few months." He tapped his solar plexus with a fist. "Just come on by the station when you get a chance, and we'll talk some more." He winked, handed over the champagne, and walked away.

Mr. Piccione and Irene Scott brought up the rear, making their way over in their usual slow hurry. Lily bent to embrace them and accept their hugs and kisses.

Then Rex clicked his way to her and jumped up, paws resting on her thighs. Lily kissed the top of his head, and as she did, a woman's voice, as delicate as the flutter of a butterfly's wings, whispered, "I love you." She could have easily missed those words if they hadn't caught her at the right moment, a moment when her heart was open.

Lily spun around in search of her sister; perhaps she would see her after all. But all she saw was her precious diner filled with the people she loved.

And that was good enough.

~ About the Author ~

Jeanne Bannon has worked in the publishing industry for over twenty-five years, first as a freelance journalist, then as an in-house editor for LexisNexis. She currently works as a freelance editor and writer.

Her debut novel, *Invisible*, a young adult paranormal romance, was published by Solstice Publishing in 2011. *Invisible* is an Amazon bestseller both domestically and internationally.

In 2014, *Beautiful Monster, The Exchange (Book One)* was released. Jeanne is finishing up work on the second in the *Beautiful Monster* series.

When not reading or writing, Jeanne enjoys spending time with her daughters, Nina and Sara and her husband, David. She's also the proud mother of two fur babies, a cuddly and affectionate Boston Terrier named Lila and Spencer, a rambunctious tabby, who can be a very bad boy.

Discover more about Jeanne Bannon here:

Twitter: @JeanneBannon
Facebook: http://www.facebook.com/pages/Jeanne-Bannon/182120961844916
Website: http://jdn022.wix.com/jeannebannon

Made in the USA
Charleston, SC
06 October 2015